Captured By Hunter

Copyright © 2025 DD DAVIS

Second Edition

DEDICATION

To those who have more love to give than they have ever received. You deserve what you put out into the world.

ACKNOWLEDGMENTS

To all my wonderful readers: thank you for your incredible support—and even more so for your saint-like patience. I know this book took a tiny bit longer to arrive than planned (okay, maybe more than a tiny bit), but you waited like champs. Whether you passed the time rereading my old work, stress-baking cookies, or just wondering if I'd been abducted by plot bunnies, I appreciate you sticking with me. This one's for you.

CONTENTS

CHAPTER 1

The first Wednesday of the month was a special day, one that she cherished above many things. It was a time for relaxation and recharging, where she could let go of the outside world and all its troubles for a few brief hours. She would reconnect with people she loved dearly over a hearty meal and strengthen the bond that they created. Each time they came together, Gianna counted herself lucky to have such amazing people in her life.

The tradition had started accidently some eight years ago after her aunt, Angela, had retired from her long career in civil service for the State of California. Zia Angela never married, so with no children or spouse to look after, she decided to spend the rest of her days traveling. She zipped around the world, taking in all that she had wanted to in her youth, but always managed to return by the beginning of the month. As Zia Angela was the only family that Gianna and her sister had, they made a habit of clearing their schedules to have dinner with her.

Those nights of laughing and talking over glasses of wine and delicious food were some of her happiest memories. Zia Angela had always brought them joy and loved them unconditionally. She paid a price for it, and it was just another of the many reasons why she was so dear to Gianna and Emilia.

When she passed away from a sudden heart attack three years ago, Gianna and Emilia promised to honor her, and the family that they created, by continuing the tradition.

And so, the first Wednesday of every month, they came together to keep the tradition, and her memory, alive.

Despite the slow moving, stop and go traffic going down I-5 South toward Greenhaven, Gianna hummed enthusiastically to 90s jams. It was nearly five in the evening, so the traffic was to be expected. She didn't mind it, however, and it wasn't just due to the fact that she was going to spend some much-desired time with her family.

She loved taking in the breathtaking, towering evergreens that lined the freeway mile after mile. Trees that had for a long time cemented the Capital as the City of Trees. As a child born and raised in the city, she had always looked up at those trees in fascination, feeling like she was traveling through a green fantasy. In some ways, she guessed she still did.

Though Sacramento was declared "America's Farm-to-Fork Capital" in recent years, she still held the old name close to her heart.

Gianna eased her little hot chocolate colored Mini Cooper off the freeway and cruised down the surface streets. Smiling to herself, she paid little attention to the Pocket-Greenhaven community where homes here were far from cookie cutter, showcasing the unique architecture of the 1970s. Lines and lines of even more evergreens that had likely towered over the streets for nearly one hundred years were a sight to see.

She parked on the right side of the driveway before climbing out of the car. Absently, she brushed away creases in her black pencil skirt after she stood. Tossing back wavy, brunette hair, she walked to her trunk to retrieve the cupcakes she had bought from a co-worker's side business. Snagging her purse and another bag, she hefted her desert up and made her way up the walkway.

Letting herself in to her sister's home, Gianna felt the stress of the past month melt away. She felt that she lived a life with an appropriate level of work-related stress, so the physical sense of calm she felt on these days always surprised her. She hadn't even begun to fully relax, but she could already feel her mood improving. The cool air from the air conditioner, working hard to combat the hot, September day, caressed her skin as the warmth of pure joy filled her heart and soul. The tantalizing scent of herbs and spices made her mouth water, beckoning her into the kitchen.

"Knock, knock!" she called, kicking the door shut behind her.

"In the kitchen!" her sister responded.

After setting her bag and dessert on the wooden console, Gianna slipped out of her heels and tossed her purse on the coat rack. She was just about to pick up her things when she made eye contact with the dazzling, smiling photo of Zia Angela. The large portrait of a Zia was taken for her sixty-fifth birthday. She looked dazzling with her silver-streaked chestnut and olive skin. Shaking her head, she obediently placed the shoes neatly under the console, just as her Zia would have wanted. It was silly, she knew, but it was little things like keeping the entryway clear of clutter that made her feel like her Zia was still with her.

She heard her phone buzz and remembering that she was waiting to hear from one of her best friends about her meeting with her ex, she quickly searched through her purse for it. Retrieving it, she eagerly read the messages, disappointed that London still hadn't responded. It was just their friend Valerie asking for an update, equally as impatient as Gianna was for news.

London had broken up with her idiot of a boyfriend, Tony, a few months ago. But she had agreed to meet with him to clear the air because he was best friends with Valerie's husband. The fall out would certainly make get togethers awkward, so it was smart of him to want to set up a truce of sorts between them before Valerie's Labor Day Party. Unfortunately, it was the only smart thing Tony had done, considering he completely botched their relationship in the first place, hurting London in a way that she hadn't seen in a long time.

Still, as angry as she was, Gianna knew that they both still had feelings for each other, so she secretly hoped that they worked it out. Besides, a happier Tony would be much more fun to beat up.

It was only a little before 5:30, and they had met at 4:30, so it was reasonable to expect a response by then but maybe it was too early to tell the outcome. Their falling out had been pretty epic, after all. She could deduce from London's lack of response that they were at least talking.

Gianna put her phone into the grocery bag before picking it and the cupcakes up to walk to the kitchen.

It was a humble space in the typical u-shaped configuration with a peninsula island of many modern kitchens. The cabinets were the same maple colored wood as the console in the entryway. The counters and backsplash were a bright white, the appliances stainless steel. The walls were a calm, light sage. Gianna set the cupcakes on the counter and pulled out the loaf of Italian bread from the grocery bag.

Emilia Johnson stood at the stove with her daughter, Ciara, gently coaching her as she stirred the pot of spaghetti sauce. Though Emilia was older by two years, their faces were nearly the same. Emilia also had brunette hair, but her waves bounced lightly in the bob haircut. She wore a white, floral halter neck blouse and black capris under an apron covered with dogs wearing glasses. In her element, she glanced over in greeting before gently nudging Ciara.

Red box braids flowing down her back, Ciara turned carefully and slowly walked to Gianna, carrying a spoonful of the delicious sauce.

"Here, aunty. You taste it." Her brown eyes landed on the dessert and lit up. "Ooh! Cupcakes!"

"I thought we agreed no cake?" Emilia asked dryly, her eyes narrowing in annoyance.

"Which is why I brought cupcakes. Aunty knows best!" Gianna replied before accepting the spoon to taste. "Oh, mmm. That's incredible."

Ciara's eyes brightened with her smile. "Seriously? Mamma said it was okay, but…"

Gianna grinned. At twelve years old, Ciara was coming into her independence, but was still a bit shy about it.

"Seriously. Let's slather this baby with butter and garlic and get to eating."

"You know where the supplies are," Emilia said. "Ciara, go ahead and put the noodles in the pot. Your mom should be here soon too."

"Okay."

Dressed in a loose shirt and shorts, Ciara glided to the pantry for the noodles. Gianna marveled for a moment at how fast her niece had grown in the short two years since Emilia and Sam adopted her. She realized now that she had focused more on her emotional and mental growth than the physical. When had her legs and arms gotten so long? And even with the loose shirt, she could tell that Emilia had been right about needing those training bras. Like Sam, Ciara had a beautiful heart shaped face and rich brown skin. Ciara didn't yet have her mom's height, but there was no telling what puberty would bring.

Shaking her head, Gianna found the butter that Emilia had put out for her and got to work.

Emilia sat in one of the stools at the peninsula. "What were you doing by the door? Talking to Zia?"

Gianna grinned. "Only briefly. I was checking my phone. London's meeting up with her ex right now."

"They're getting back together?"

"If that idiot man knows what's good for him, he'll be begging and pleading for just that."

"You heteros are so messy."

Gianna cackled. "As if you weren't before Sam changed your entire world."

Emilia leaned back in the stool, grinning and thinking of her wife. "Got me there."

"Is she showing a house?"

"Yeah," Emilia said before getting up to open a bottle of red wine. "Last minute request or she would have been here already. She said she's on her way though."

"Traffic was trafficking."

Emilia snorted. "Figures."

Ciara took Emilia's seat and watched her open the bottle. "I thought you didn't like London's boyfriend."

"I didn't like that he hurt London," Gianna corrected. She turned to put the bread in the oven before continuing. "But love is messy."

"And family is messier," Emilia added as she poured three glasses.

Ciara nodded in understanding, knowing all too well that what they said was true. "Sometimes the family you make is better."

Gianna wrapped her arm around Ciara's waist and leaned into her. "You're absolutely right. Maybe their family will stay together, or maybe they'll make one of their own. I just want them both to be happy."

"Do you…" Ciara bit her lip, hesitating before gathering her courage. "Do you ever wish things were different with your parents?"

"No. Not even once," Gianna answered honestly. "Emilia?"

"I used to," she answered, happy that Ciara felt comfortable asking, even at the risk of the topic being a painful one. "I used to wish they could love me for who I am and not who they wanted me to be. But I had Gianna and Zia Angela and many other people who helped me realize that it's their loss and not mine."

When Ciara only nodded in response, Gianna rubbed her arm.

"What about you? Do you wish things were

different with your parents? With your family?"

Ciara leaned into her. "No. I'm exactly where I need to be."

Sam entered the kitchen from the garage then, breaking what little tension there was and filling the space with even more love. Her snappy suit was a solid blue, contrasting her blond hair that was shaved in a beautiful taper. Her eyes twinkled in delight when she stepped up to Emilia for a kiss. She put her purse down to envelope Ciara in a long hug.

"Hi, baby. Can't wait to hear about school."

"It was okay."

"Uh huh," she teased before hugging Gianna. "Why are there cupcakes on my counter?"

"I'm not sure why you psychos actually thought I'd agree to skip desert."

They jokingly argued as they made their plates. Laughed at descriptions of the homes and buildings Sam and Emilia had shown that month as they ate. While eating second helpings, they grumbled and pouted along with Ciara over pop quizzes and upcoming assignments. They chatted about tv shows, music, and more as they simply enjoyed each other's company.

Gianna talked more with Ciara as they tag teamed the kitchen clean up, giving Emilia and Sam a moment to themselves. Then they all came back to the table for desert and the monthly family meeting.

"I want to grow our family."

All eyes landed on Sam in silence at this announcement. Per the rules of their family meeting, only Sam could speak until she placed the squat figurine of an Italian chef that Zia Angela had picked up in Venice at the center of the table. She held it in both hands, her thumbs absently rubbing its sides.

"I'm happy," she clarified. "So happy with what we have here. But there's more I want to give you, Ciara. I want you to have a brother or a sister. I want to take our little family of four to sit in pairs on rollercoasters. Get a cabin on a cruise. A family of four is what I've always pictured myself with."

She paused a moment to let it sink in before continuing with what she felt would be the hardest part of all of this.

"We would need to move. I want a bigger house, something we can renovate into exactly what we want. Into exactly what you want," she said, meeting Ciara's eyes directly. "Moving would affect you the most. I'm sorry. You've finally gotten used to being here with us and I'm asking you to change. It's selfish of me to ask this of you."

Sam sighed before continuing. "I know this has to be something we all agree on. Ciara, you'll have the biggest say. Then Emilia. Gianna, you'll likely have to do interviews again if we decide to move forward, so you needed to know."

Sam took a deep breath before scanning the faces of those she loved.

"It's a big decision. Since it is, we won't discuss it until next month's meeting. We each think about it on our own. Weigh the pros and cons, consider our hopes and fears. We won't make a decision to adopt unless all are agreed and we will respect anyone who doesn't want to."

Sam pushed the little figurine into the center of the table. Normally, they would hash things out during their meeting, but when a big topic like this came up, they would sit on it until the next month to ensure everyone made their decision with a clear conscience.

Gianna could see that everyone was already thinking about it, the wheels turning in their heads as they stared at the figurine. Wanting to ease the tension, she reached in to pick it up.

"Since that's a heavy topic, I'm requesting a heavy meal and a heavy desert next month. I'm thinking Zia's lasagna and Sam's banana pudding."

Sam gave her a weak smile, appreciating her effort to bring them back down to Earth. "How about peach cobbler?"

"Even better."

∞∞∞∞∞∞∞

Gianna drove in silence on the long drive from Greenhaven to her condo in Folsom. Her thoughts, however, were far from quiet.

There were so many feelings and ideas and thoughts on this potential big change for her sister's family. If they did decide to adopt and move, she hoped that they would move closer, so she didn't have to make such a long drive to see them.

As soon as she had the idea, she rolled her eyes at her own foolishness and selfishness. Out of her thirty years of living, she had lived with her sister in some capacity for twenty-five of them. Of the remaining five years, they lived a mere fifteen-minute drive apart for three of them. This forty-minute drive was the farthest they had ever been apart.

Wanting to close that distance made her feel just a little bit pathetic.

Gianna and Emilia had always been close, and the fallout with their DNA providers brought them even closer. After graduating from high school and being kicked out by said DNA providers, Emilia moved in with Zia Angela. Soon after, Zia purchased the condo in Folsom. Gianna moved in with them a year later after her emancipation was approved. The years that followed, she and Emilia lived and struggled together as they worked to become self-sufficient and educated adults.

For Gianna, that meant attending classes at Folsom Lake College and working as a student assistant for the State. Eventually, she was able to transfer to Sacramento State University to get her Bachelors in Computer Engineering as well as land a full-time position in the IT office at the California Department of Fish and Wildlife.

Emilia attended FLC as well, but since she had spent most of her childhood trying to be what and who their DNA providers wanted her to be, it took her a lot longer to find who she wanted to be and what she wanted to do with her life. Eventually, she obtained a degree in Business Admin and her real estate license.

After Emilia met and married Sam, Sam moved in with Emilia in Folsom and Gianna took over Sam's lease at an apartment in Rancho Cordova, which was only fifteen-minutes away. They had planned to live out their lives in that condo, doing renovations and other improvements so that space fit their needs, but all that changed when they decided to adopt.

Gianna respected and admired their reasons for moving. After meeting and deciding to adopt Ciara, who had been in and out of the foster care system for far too long, Emilia and Sam hadn't wanted to change the one thing that had stayed consistent for her. So, they purchased a home in Greenhaven so that Ciara could stay in the same school district and neighborhood that she had lived in for the last seven years.

Would they make a decision like that again? she wondered. If they clicked with a child that lived in a different neighborhood, would they move there to make the transition easier for them? How would Ciara feel about that? Or would they choose a house that worked for all of them regardless of how that move would impact their children?

She didn't envy the complicated journey they were about to make, but she would be there for them every step of the way. While pathetically wishing they moved closer to her.

Gianna pulled into the garage of her two-story condo, waiting until the door fully closed before climbing out of the car to retrieve her purse, laptop backpack, and leftovers. She kicked her shoes off, too tired to store them properly, as she unlocked her door.

The moment she stepped inside and turned on the lights, she was nearly tripped by her brown Bengal cat, Shrek, who mewled in annoyance as he wove between her legs.

"Okay, baby. I know. I was gone for so long," she soothed as she walked to her small round, dining table to drop her bags. Hands free, she scooped him up in her arms for a hug. "Where's your princess, hmm? Hasn't she been keeping you company?"

Shrek bumped his head against her chin before jumping down to lead the way. He didn't go far for Fiona sat demurely next to an empty food bowl behind the peninsula. She gave one quiet meow and a swish of her tail in greeting., clearly indicating that no love would be shown until she received her dinner.

Rolling her eyes, Gianna glided into her kitchen. Once upon a time, the dining room had been where the kitchen now stood, but that was before Emilia and Sam. The U-shaped kitchen allowed her to see over the peninsula and into her living room. Here the cabinets were a navy blue with white quartz countertops and stainless-steel appliances.

She opened the pantry and retrieved a can of wet cat food. Shrek shamelessly whined for his meal as she scooped the food into two bowls. After placing the bowls next to their water, she picked up the old bowls and placed them in the sink. Then she went back to the dining room nook and unpacked her things.

Moving upstairs, she stepped into her owner's suite to prepare for bed, her thoughts still unsettled. She wiggled her back as an invisible itch danced between her shoulders. It was time for a change. So many people in her life were moving forward with their own. Growing or making changes, their thoughts on the future. It was time for her to do the same. She realized now that she still felt a bit stuck even after moving to Intel. She had been so sure that it was the change that she needed, but there was still something missing.

Staring at her reflection as she removed her makeup, Gianna wondered what her own future would hold. And more importantly, she wondered how she could shape it into something that would make her happy.

With her thoughts swirling, she finished getting ready for bed even though she was sure that it would be a long, sleepless night.

CHAPTER 2

London finally responded just as she was crawling into bed later that night, but provided no details around her conversation with Tony. Instead, she requested that they meet up after work so she could give them all the details in person. They settled on meeting downtown so that Tony could swing by and pick her up after they were done with dinner.

With seeing Tony in mind, Gianna dressed that morning with the intent to be able to comfortably take a few swings at him. Dressed in loose, high waist wide leg trousers in black, a vivid red cropped sweater vest, and matching red shoes, she crossed the street with a determined and eager swagger.

Behind her, the vibrant DOCO sign glowed with the Golden 1 Center as its backdrop. The temporary outdoor Downtown Sacramento Roller Rink was a new addition to the downtown commons, and one she had yet to try. She would be sure to bring it up to her friends to see if they could get down there before it closed at the end of September.

Restaurants and bars lined the pedestrian street mall named The Kay. Though the mall went on for seven blocks down K Street, Darling Aviary was just a few stores down from where she crossed the street.

Darling Aviary was a stunning bar, with rooftop dining space for the restaurant. After getting carded at the door, she stepped into the dimly lit bar. Bottles lined the brick walls on lighted shelves, as if glowing with excitement to be poured. Lights underneath the bar spotlighted low back stools covered in rich, emerald green velvet, beckoning patrons to sit comfortably and enjoy. A human-sized bird cage sat in the back, further showcasing the avian theme.

Cool air and thumping beats enveloped her as she stepped inside. She wasn't looking for it, but she felt the weight of someone's gaze on her. Her eyes swept casually to her left, landing briefly on two men posted at the bar. Both had turned slightly in her direction, their conversation momentarily paused, their smirks half-formed like they had already exchanged some silent agreement.

Uninterested, she walked to the elevator and pressed the call button.

The doors opened and she went inside. One of the men joined her and tried to catch her eye, but she simply stared ahead. Any other day, she might have entertained him, and herself, but over the last few months, she simply hadn't been interested in playing the usual game of cat and mouse with men. She could attribute some of the disinterest to focusing on getting settled at Intel and ensuring that she passed her six-month probationary period.

But mostly, she just didn't feel inclined to make space even a casual fling.

Between work, family, friends, gaming, martial arts and running her non-profit, she had more than enough to keep her occupied. And after witnessing all the drama Valerie and London went through with the men in their lives, she really didn't understand how they managed it all. Life was much simpler being single.

When the elevator doors slid open, the man stepped out and casually threw an arm across the threshold to keep them from closing. For the first time, she gave him more than a passing glance and immediately smirked. Everything about him, from the messy blond hair to the loud graphic tee and overconfident stance, screamed frat boy who never graduated, trapped in the body of a man pretending to have it all together.

Labeling him so quickly made her realize that London's behavior was finally starting to rub off her. Amused, she stepped off the elevator and murmured her thanks.

"You're welcome," he said with an inviting smile. "Can I get you a drink?"

"That's sweet of you, but unnecessary. Have a good night."

His expression immediately darkened, but he quickly plastered on another smile. He followed her determinedly down the hall and out to the rooftop area where several green triangular sails were hung up above to provide relief from the sun. Narrow wood and stainless-steel tables filled the space. Nearly every stool and table were taken, she noted, as she scanned for her friends, ignoring Frat Boy.

"How about your number then?"

Gianna found her friends, but didn't want him following her over so she turned to him and gave him her best smile, still trying to be polite.

"I could, but it would be fake," she confessed. "So, let's just skip past that whole disappointment, okay?

Have a good night."

She left him with a surprised look on his face. Weaving through the tables, she finally made it to her friends who had found a table in the farthest back corner. Alarmingly, London looked more dejected than happy. She clutched Valerie's hand tightly over the table and looked up with a weak smile when she saw Gianna.

"I'll kill him," she said immediately, her entire body vibrating with rage.

"Wait!" Valerie grabbed her arm as she turned to leave. "Just wait. Sit down, John Wick. Your services aren't needed this time."

"What happened?" Gianna demanded, sitting down and placing her hand over London and Valerie's. "I thought you worked things out."

"We did, but—"

She was cut off when their drinks arrived. One of Darling Aviary's claim to fame were their drinks, and the three the waitress dropped off looked like they would live up to the hype. They were also known for their hamburgers so they ordered some and a few other items to share before diving back in to their conversation.

London took a small sip to calm herself before she told them about running into Mr. Cheng, Tony's dad, something that had surprised them both. She smiled and laughed as she detailed her panic upon finding that she had walked into a carefully crafted trap designed by someone who knew her well before finally accepting that they could be together, no matter what his parents thought. Thankfully, their relationship wouldn't cause a rift between Tony and his family, but that didn't explain why she wasn't bubbling over with joy.

"As soon as he drove into his parking garage, my heart started racing. At first, I thought I was just excited. It had been so long since we were together. But as he held me on the elevator ride up, my hands got clammy. By the time we got to his apartment, I was shaking. The last time I was there was when I realized I was in love with him. Going back there after he broke it the very next day…"

She paused to take another drink before continuing. "The second I stepped inside his apartment and looked around, I fell apart. Just completely lost it. Sobbing uncontrollably while he tried to figure out what was wrong. We sat on the couch and he held me while I cried for what felt like forever. I remember him apologizing over and over. When I finally calmed down, he offered to call you two, to take me home, and I cried again. Staying hurt, but the thought of leaving hurt more."

"Oh, honey," Gianna whispered, squeezing her hand tighter.

"I fell asleep at some point and woke up, alone, in his bed. After a shower and some coffee, I felt a little bit more myself. We sat in silence for a while, not knowing what to say to each other. Eventually I told him that I would need time."

"You're breaking up?" Valerie asked.

London shook her head in denial. "I'm so desperately in love with him, but I also have all this hurt that I still need time to move past. I thought that time away from him had healed me, but boy was I wrong. We just agreed to take things slow, ease back into things instead of trying to pick up where we left off."

"We?" Gianna asked, her voice tinted with anger.

"Or him? Is he pushing you to do this?"

"It's more my idea than his, actually. He thought I was going to leave him."

"You should," Gianna agreed, trying to wrap her head around London's insistence that they stay together while their food was delivered.

"Maybe," London responded after a moment. "But love is…complicated."

"And messy," she added, thinking of her conversation with Emilia and Ciara last night. "Uhm, this chicken burger is fucking delicious."

London laughed. "One of the reasons why I wanted to come here."

"Should we be happy for you?" Valerie asked, her voice unsure.

"Yes. Even through all of that pain, it still felt so right to be there with him. We both called out and we just sat with each other for half the day. No kissing, no sex. An occasional light, tentative brush or touch every now and then. It's just going to take a bit of time to rebuild the intimacy and trust."

Gianna gave a frustrated sigh. "I've never wanted to beat someone up so bad."

London chuckled. "He looks worse than I do. Trust me, he's beating himself up plenty."

"I'll let these hands be the judge."

"We're never going to hear the end of this," Valerie said with a sigh.

"That's correct. Not until I hurt him. Physically," she added when she noticed London was about to speak. "Just one kick to the balls at least! It's not like either of you are planning to use them anytime soon."

London snorted out a laugh. "Gawd, you're a mess."

"I'm telling you. Both of you would feel a whole lot better if you just…"

Gianna mimed a few backhands, elbows, slaps and punches, sending the two into a laughing fit.

"You can't fool me with this tough girl act, Gianna Maffucci," London clucked her tongue. "Once you get a look at him tonight, you'll realize that hitting him would be just as vile as kicking a sick puppy."

Gianna pouted. "You are no fun."

Valerie patted her hand. "We'll find someone else for you to pick on."

"Hunter?" London asked, her eyebrows wiggling suggestively.

Gianna snorted in response.

"Hunter? Who? Wait," Valerie threw her hands up in surprise. "My cousin Hunter?"

"Yep."

"No," Gianna said at the same time. "Ignore her."

"She practically gobbled him up with her eyes at your wedding," London tattled with a wide grin.

"Oh…wow," Valerie said, trying to process this new information. "I had no idea."

"Oh my gosh. Stop! There's nothing. That was my first time seeing Hunter since high school. I didn't recognize him and thought he had a decent body. That in no way means what London is trying to suggest."

"Did you talk to him at the wedding?"

"Only when London dragged me over to him."

"Where you promptly tried flirting with him, but he wasn't having any of it," London explained.

Valerie's eyes widened in surprise, trying to process the fact that her best friend flirted with her cousin and he remained unaffected. The only men she knew who weren't immediately charmed by Gianna were all taken.

She knew Hunter to be single. Maybe he had a type that she didn't know about. London would know better than she would.

"I flirt with everyone, remember?"

"Hah! Who are you trying to fool with that high school lie? Certainly not us," London said, sending her a knowing look.

Gianna shrugged. "It doesn't matter. He clearly has incredibly poor taste anyway. That's his problem not mine."

"Isn't he going to be at your party of Sunday, Valerie?"

"Yes," she confirmed. "Ever since that car accident, he's been trying to spend more time with anyone he considers family."

"At least there was a little bit of good to come out of it. Gianna," London said as she looked over. "You'll have more opportunities to try flirting with him again."

Gianna rolled her eyes. "Pass. Oh, but speaking of Sunday. Are you okay if I show up early? I'm tutoring in Natomas that morning."

"Carla's sister?" Valerie asked, remembering that she had given Gianna's number to a previous student's parents.

"No, another girl that I've been tutoring for a while. I'm meeting with Carla's sister next week though."

"Alright. That's no problem, but don't complain if I put you to work."

"Not even. Are you sure we don't need to bring anything?"

"Ruben and Maya are handing the food," Valerie said, speaking of her older brother and sister-in-law. "Jun and I are handling the entertainment."

"I can't wait," Gianna confessed and then looked

over at London. "Do we have time for another story?"

"Yeah," she answered. "Tony and Jun said they'll come by when we're ready for them, so no rush. What's up?"

"Well, I got an interesting email from the parent of a former client this afternoon," Gianna explained as she pushed aside her plate. "I tutored her daughter, Hailey, in middle school and now she's a high school junior. Talking about college."

"Wow. Time flies," Valerie said.

"Exactly! I had to take a moment to accept how old I'm getting," Gianna pouted. "Anyway. Hailey is pretty sure she wants to go into computer engineering so her mom reached out to see if I knew of any STEM specific scholarships. On the ride here, I tried to recall some of the ones I applied for and something crazy occurred to me."

"Excuse me, ladies," the waitress interrupted with a tray of drinks. "Some drinks from the guy at the bar. His number is on the napkin."

They all glanced toward the bar where Frat Boy was perched, his face flushed with alcohol. He sent them a look that Gianna was sure he meant to be sexy, but he just looked creepy instead. Beside him, an African American guy said something and seemed to shake his head in embarrassment.

"Gianna strikes again," Valerie said with a grin.

"I already shot him down," Gianna said with a roll of her eyes.

London lifted an eyebrow in surprise. "You're not going to talk to him? He's kind of cute."

"Sure, in a frat boy who hasn't grown up kind of way."

Valerie laughed. "He did kind of have that vibe.

Rich frat boy vibe is strong with that one."

"We've both been hanging out with this one too much," Gianna declared, pointing at London before turning to the waitress. "Please tell him absolutely nothing, but thank the bartender for the drink," she told the waitress. "Anyway. The STEM scholarships."

"And crazy ideas," London reminded her.

"I think I want to offer my own STEM scholarship. Specifically for women, obviously, through my non-profit."

"Uhm," Valerie said. "That's not crazy. That's brilliant!"

Men and drinks forgotten, they talked it out before easing into relaxed conversation. Though they talked nearly all day in their group chat, they never ran out of things to talk about. As the sun finally began to set on the city, they paid the bill and made their way downstairs.

It was busier inside the restaurant and bar now. Every seat at the bar was nearly taken, mostly by who she assumed were friends of the two men she had seen down there before. It was a fairly large group of them, and judging from some of their casual and dirty attire, many of them had come straight there from some sort of construction job.

Frat Boy saw them coming and downed a shot before weaving over to her, more intoxicated than he had been upstairs, and blocked the exit.

"Back again? Give me your number. Hot girl like you? I'd take real good care of you."

Gianna swung an annoyed stare at his friends. The African American man from earlier took the hint and tried pulling him out of the way. He managed to create enough space for London and Valerie to get by before

Frat Boy shrugged him off.

"The answer is still no," she said, smiling brightly as she gently pushed him towards his friends. "Have a good night."

"Stupid bitch. You'll regret this. Women like you always do when they realize I'm the best thing they'll never have."

Thankfully, despite his protesting, his friends managed to hold on to him long enough for her to get away. When she stepped outside, London and Valerie were waiting off to the side.

"That was…cute," London said.

"If so cute, why hesitation?"

Her friend merely grinned. "Usually, you play with them a little bit longer than that. What gives?"

"Not interested. I'm holding out for a nice, sexy Asian guy like my besties. I'll be celibate until then."

Valerie laughed. "Wouldn't that be funny if we all ended up with Asian guys?"

"Speaking of sexy Asian men," London said, turning toward DOCO.

Gianna followed her gaze until her eyes landed on a pair of attractive Asian men. Jun chatted animatedly, his hands moving, his long black hair dancing wildly behind his back as he walked toward them.

Beside him was Tony, who was looking at them with guarded and tired eyes. Though he wore blue slacks and a white collared shirt that he had tucked in, both fit him loosely, like they were a size too large. As he came closer, she saw that there were bags under his eyes and he looked just a little bit sickly.

His attention focused solely on London when they reached them, and while his eyes lit up with longing, there was pain there too. He reached out to her, the move more cautious than bold, and lightly brushed a hand down her arm before pulling away again.

"Hi," London said quietly, almost shyly. "You went in after all?"

"Hi. Yeah, I had a few things to handle," he added, before turning to speak to her friends. "Hi, Valerie. Hi, Gianna. I'm sorry."

Gianna snorted, annoyed with his appearance. He really did look like a sick puppy. How could she smack him around when he apologized with that sad look on his face?

"You look like shit."

Tony smiled weakly. "Feel like it too. Well-deserved since I hurt London and broke my word."

"Smelled like shit too until I made his ass get in the shower," Jun added, wrapping his arm around Valerie's waist with a smug look on his face.

"I'll make it up to you," Tony said, ignoring his friend. He took London's hand and stared into her eyes. "Anything I can do to make it up to you, I'll do it."

"We'll figure it out as we go," London said, fighting back tears. "Let's go to my place."

"Okay," he said, letting her lead him away. He stopped suddenly and turned back to Gianna. "I'm really sorry."

She sighed and waved him away. "Yeah, yeah. I'm still going to kick your ass later, so just focus on making it up to her so you're both not acting like wounded dogs."

Jun grinned as he watched them walk away. "I'm a little disappointed that you didn't kick his ass. You have amazing restraint."

"Good things come to those who wait."

Valerie shook her head. "Want us to walk you to your car?"

"Nah. I'm just in the garage across the street. I'll see you Saturday."

It didn't take her long to get back to her car, and for the second night in a row, she rode in silence on the way home. This time, her thoughts were consumed with the messiness of love. She had to assume it was all worth it, but why couldn't love just come easy? All the mess and heartache and stress. She didn't want to experience any of it. She simply wanted love in its purest, most powerful, unconditional form without any of the hassle it took to get there.

She hadn't been in love before. She didn't have a past with a long list of relationships that ended with heartbreak, despite all the dating she did. She enjoyed men, their company, sex, but she never let anyone get close enough to her to earn the title of boyfriend. To earn her love. She got to know someone well enough to feel comfortable letting them scratch an itch, and once she was satisfied enough, she ended things and moved on.

As much as she wanted love, she had no desire to go through what London and Valerie did. She had yet to meet a man who made her feel like all the trouble was worth it. If that type of man was out there, she hadn't met him yet.

She just had to resist the urge to believe that he wasn't out there at all.

CHAPTER 3

Jamming to Queen in her car, Gianna glanced at the clock as she pulled in front of Valerie and Jun's for their Labor Day Party a little later than she had intended. She hadn't anticipated her tutoring session running over. Should have, she thought ruefully as she reached across the car to retrieve her purse. She had a reputation for always running late, and while most assumed, much to her annoyance, that it was because she spent too much time on her looks, it was rarely, if ever, the reason.

She was an extrovert, through and through. There was nothing she liked more than being with people. As a result, she always got caught up in conversations, and it had an unfortunate domino effect on her day. She could, quite easily, be on time for the first item on her agenda that day, be it work, a meeting, an appointment, or an event. But she usually ended up being late for anything that followed.

This morning had been no exception, and she had absolutely no regrets. Grinning with joy and excitement, she pulled out her brush to do something to the wild curls she hadn't bothered to tame before she left that morning. Tammy had made quite the breakthrough this morning, and it had demanded more than their hour session.

All summer, Gianna had been tutoring Tammy, soon to be tenth grader at Natomas High School, after she received a barely passing grade in Algebra I in June. She could see early on that Tammy's hate and disdain for math stemmed mostly from her own belief that she would never be good at math.

Two months of trying to show Tammy that she was much brighter than she gave herself credit for, Gianna finally witnessed the moment the young girl believed it herself.

After completing a worksheet, Tammy began to check her answers. There had been a moment of frustration in her eyes when she found an incorrect answer, but unlike the other times, Gianna hadn't seen it accompanied with a frown of defeat.

Instead, Tammy started over, a stubborn determination lighting her eyes as she reworked the problem. And then her eyes brightened, her body seemed to snap to attention as not only the answer became clear, but also the why and how she made the mistake in the first place and what she should have done instead.

Gianna had said nothing when Tammy grabbed and quickly completed another worksheet. Then she looked up at Gianna, joy and shock and confidence and pleasure filling her eyes. Her words spilled out a mile a minute as she walked Gianna through the revelation that she had just uncovered. They ended up spending the next thirty minutes talking about other math concepts before Gianna realized that their session was over.

She knew all too well what it was like to think you

weren't any good at math for no other reason than your gender. She had been just like Tammy in middle and high school, and it wasn't until she saw a tutor that things had changed and she learned that she actually really liked math. Her life was never the same afterward.

As she climbed out of her car, she glanced at Valerie's brother's house, which was right next door and took note of the large pick-up truck that sat in the driveway. She had never seen this truck before and wondered if Ruben had crossed over to truck life.

The combination of thinking of her own math tutor and Ruben made her think of his cousin, Hunter. The two of them were similar in height and coloring, so it wasn't that much of a stretch, but she hadn't seen or thought of the statuesque man since Hawaii. Or rather, since London had brought him up at dinner a few days ago. Since their interactions hadn't been exactly friendly, there hadn't been a need to think about him.

The tall, handsome, and muscular man had been easy on the eyes but hard to be around. Their interaction after they literally bumped into each other still baffled her when she actually thought about it again. He had been rude and uncaring, blaming their accidental collision on her while her ears rang from the impact. After she called him out on it, and stopped him from saying something sexist, his tune changed a little.

When he finally checked on her, he had been rougher than she would have liked, but there had also been something oddly gentle and caring in his actions.

She remembered their eyes meeting, and the feeling of warmth from where he held her chin. Warmth that had traveled through her body until it burst from the tips of her fingers and toes. Her heart rate had sped up in response.

Had his eyes flicked down to look at her lips, or had that been her imagination? She definitely hadn't missed the moment he withdrew, physically and emotionally. His eyes had frosted over, turned hard and angry before he stepped away from her.

The interaction had left her more than a little confused, and she gave him space for the remainder of their time in Hawaii. She was almost positive that he didn't like her, and she had no idea why. They had always been friendly in high school, and he and Ruben were the only boys that she had been comfortable around during those years. So why did he react that way to her?

The once shy, sweet, math genius had completely changed her life. The woman she became was because he tutored her, and this new phase of her business she hoped to take would have the same life alternating impact that his assistance had on hers. She owed it to him to thank him, to show him that his efforts hadn't been for nothing.

Whatever the problem was between them, she wanted to fix it so she could thank him properly. Liking the idea, she knocked lightly on Valerie's door before letting herself in. She kicked off her shoes and placed them on the bench inside of the entryway closet. Walking to the kitchen, she noticed that the bold, black accent wall that had once held photos of the places Jun had traveled actually had people in them now. Photos of Jun and Valerie, and the two families they had brought together. Such a simple yet grand change brought a smile to her face.

Jun was walking to the door when she came in. "Hello, gorgeous."

Gianna winked at him. "Hey, handsome. Where's my girl?"

"She's helping Maya carry some of the food over here. Grab your shoes. I'll walk you over this way."

She turned back to do that. "I can make it on my own. It's just next door."

"It's okay. I want to show you something."

"Oh, dear," she said, doing her best to sound patronizing. "I'm sure your grill is just a big as Ruben's."

Jun laughed. "Just wait."

Gianna followed him to the sliding glass door just off the dining room and into the backyard before stopping to put on her shoes. She stepped out onto a small concrete slab that was just big enough for a handful of chairs and a grill. The rest of the small space was freshly manicured grass. She knew it was a decent size for Natomas considering that more and more new homes were being built with zero lot lines. Some homes had a quarter of the space that Jun had.

Gianna tilted her head to the side as she took note of the large, concrete pavers that formed a walkway from Jun's slab to the fence that separated his property from Ruben's. She was just wondering about the long bar on it when the fence moved easily, as if it was on wheels, and opened up to reveal Ruben's kids, Phillip and Nathan, romping around in their own yard.

Her mouth fell open in surprise. There was suddenly no fence separating the two yards, and the feeling instead was now one long and spacious area. The same concrete pavers met in the middle and carried over to Ruben and Maya's slab, unifying the design. The attractive walkway beckoned her to sit in their chairs.

She imagined lounging on blankets in the grass. Or sitting at rows of tables and chairs as they passed conversation and food. It was too bad that it was too hot to do just that today. Still, that didn't stop the boys from taking advantage of the additional area to play tag.

Ruben leaned against the doors he had just opened and grinned. "I see Jun is still getting a kick out of people's reactions."

"You know it! Cool, isn't it?" Jun grinned.

"It's incredible! It has such a dramatic impact, opening it up like this," she said in awe. "Who did this? *How* did they do this?"

"It pays to have a family member in the construction business. You'll have to talk to Hunter on the how. I still don't get it," Ruben added with a shrug. "But that's why I could never work for my uncle."

"Hunter? Construction?" Her thoughts whirled for a moment before she remembered. "Oh! Your uncle has a business, right?"

"Yep," Ruben confirmed. "Hall Construction. Uncle Ben's retiring soon though so Hunter and Madison will be taking over."

"Well, you two are so lucky. This is absolutely fantastic."

"Definitely," Jun said in agreement. "Hunter finished it up last Friday. Well, technically, just this morning. It turned out better than he said it would."

"It's pure genius," she said, crossing over into Ruben's backyard.

Her gaze drifted over toward their backdoor where she saw a man kneeling in front of a large tool bag. His muscles flexed and bulged, brown skin glistening with sweat, as he haphazardly shoved tools back inside. Once he finished, he stood and turned to walk toward them.

Gianna felt the hum of attraction, her eyes following him as he crossed the yard with an easy, unbothered stride. He wore a faded white tee and cargo shorts that were speckled with splatters of who knew what. His goatee was just full enough to be intentional, framing his mouth in a way that made her throat go a little dry.

Then his mouth tightened as if in annoyance and she finally realized that she was openly checking him out. Disturbed, her eyes snapped up to his. Luckily, he wasn't looking at her. She sincerely hoped he hadn't noticed. It would be challenging to fix whatever was wrong between them if he thought she wanted to jump him.

Which, she didn't. Not even a little. Right?

Ruben's grin practically split his face as he looked over the yard. "You were right. Those handles made it easy for the boys to open it up. It'll be hard for us to keep them out of their yard now."

"I put a lock on both sides at the top," Hunter said quietly.

"No way? I didn't even pay attention when I opened it just now."

Ruben and Jun turned their attention back to the fence to check it out. While Gianna wasn't alone with Hunter, it was strangely exactly how she felt. It was awkward. Refusing to feel unsettled by the weird vibe between them, she offered him a friendly smile.

"Hi, Hunter. This is really impressive."

He shrugged as if it wasn't a big deal. "Thanks."

"How long have you been doing construction work?"

"Few years," he said, going back to lift the tool bag.

She had to rip her eyes away from his ass, too distracted by her own growing attraction to notice how curt he was being.

Gianna cleared her throat. "Do you have any business cards on hand? My sister may move soon and knowing her, she'll want to make changes."

"Sure."

She blinked after him as he turned abruptly and walked away. Not sure how to respond, she decided that he meant for her to follow him out the side gate to the front of the house. He climbed in the back of the pick-up truck in Ruben's drive way, unknowingly answering her question about the vehicle, and lifted the toolbox lid before placing his bag inside. He locked it and turned, seeming surprised to see her standing there.

"Uh, you meant right now?"

Gianna blinked again. "I thought you wanted me to follow you."

"I didn't say that," he said, mildly annoyed and climbed down.

"You didn't say anything, really," she said, finally noticing his less than friendly attitude toward her. "But since I've been practicing to be a mind reader, I thought I'd give it a go. Clearly, I still need some work."

He sighed. "I think I have some."

"Appreciate it," she said dryly, wondering if she should even bother.

Hunter opened his passenger door and rummaged around inside his truck for a moment.

"Here," he said, thrusting a handful of cards at her.

"Thanks," she said, even though she was feeling anything but grateful. He didn't seem like he wanted her business at all, so she felt slightly foolish for even taking them. "I'll, uh, be in touch. I guess."

Hunter immediately felt the tension leave his body after she walked away. He pulled a different bag from inside his truck and closed the door, locking it as he went inside his cousin's house. Shaking his head in annoyance, he locked himself in the downstairs bathroom that had once been used by Valerie when she lived here. He looked at his reflection in the mirror with a frown.

"You're an idiot," he told himself.

It was stupid and annoying that he still tensed up when he saw Gianna. Made sense in high school, but now that they were both adults, he didn't understand why her presence still elicited that reaction.

"You still don't like her."

He heard the declaration London had delivered at Valerie's wedding reception like she was standing next to him. Maybe it was truer than he was willing to admit, and that thought left him feeling even more confused. He hadn't seen or spoken to Gianna since he finished tutoring her during his junior year of high school. Back then, she always made him nervous and self-conscious. He never did well when it came to talking to girls, but whenever it was Gianna, those feelings were ramped up even higher. He had worked very hard in college to leave that shy kid behind.

After turning on the shower water, Hunter stripped out of his sweat-soaked clothes. He hadn't been in the backyard long, but the beating sun and 75-degree temperature was hot enough to leave him drenched.

He looked at himself in the mirror again, seeing the confident, muscled man he shaped himself to be. In place of his once thin, long arms were thick and defined biceps and triceps. A long scar ran alongside his flat stomach, which never quite developed into defined abs. He didn't mind since he was finally happy with his body and focused more on maintaining what he had than bulking up or thinning out.

No longer being the lanky, shy, and awkward boy he had been high school was all that mattered. So why did he feel himself reverting back to that in Gianna's presence?

Climbing into the shower, Hunter let the water run over his body and clear his head. His therapist would probably have something to say about this. He hadn't talked about Gianna in his last session, hadn't felt the need to, but perhaps he should next time. Sure, their first interaction in years had been a little… complicated, but it didn't make sense for it to keep being that way.

He hadn't handled that first interaction well, he admitted to himself as he lathered his body with a washcloth and soap. It was a reflection he wouldn't have been able to reach on his own a year ago, but he could now see his internalized misogyny when it showed its ugly face. His therapist had helped him uncover and address the thing that was preventing him from having healthy and satisfying relationships with women.

Things had gotten better, or at least he thought they had until he had quite literally bumped into Gianna. Her reaction to him had been entirely appropriate, while he had become immediately defensive and had definitely been more sexist than he would have liked. It had been a knee jerk reaction to accuse her of using her good looks to her advantage, but in his defense, she did have a history of doing just that.

Turning off the water after rinsing, Hunter stepped

out of the shower to dry off. He really should give her the benefit of the doubt. He wasn't the only one who had changed since high school, at least that's what he wanted to believe. He looked at his phone before getting dressed in a simple pink t-shirt and black shorts. He killed enough time that Gianna wouldn't be the only other person there besides his cousins and their partners. The fact that he was stalling, hesitant to see her again, was reason enough to bring this odd behavior to his therapist's attention.

Sighing, he shoved his dirty clothes and wet towels into his bag before pulling out his toiletries. After putting on lotion, deodorant, and cologne and brushing his hair and goatee, he shoved everything back inside and took the bag back out to his truck. He went back inside to lock up before going through the backyard to Valerie's house.

Jun was outside again, this time showing Dustin and Alena the fence set up. He waved in greeting but didn't stop to chat, having had enough of the outdoors for the day. The cold air from the AC and the delicious scent of food embraced him the moment he stepped inside of Valerie's dining room.

Only now, it wasn't set up as a dining room. The table was pushed up against the wall to his left and on it sat various games and other materials. Taped up on the wall directly in front of him was a large piece of paper with a tournament bracket drawn on it. He grinned, realizing what was going on.

Some of his favorite memories growing up were the crazy family game nights that they used to have. Getting together with his aunts, uncles and cousins to eat great food and compete in games was an amazing tradition that he hated to grow out of. Now that they were all grown up and engrossed in their own careers and lives, the family didn't get together as much as they once had in the past. He loved that Valerie wanted to bring them all back together with this tradition.

After the car accident, he was reminded of how important family and friends are. It was the reason he started making a concerted effort to spend more time with his family. Though he worked with his parents and siblings at Hall Construction, too much of their time was spent together during work hours. He missed the meaningful moments and gatherings that they typically experienced only during holiday gatherings so he insisted on having dinner with them outside of those dates. Once he got that rolling, he started inviting himself over to Ruben's more often, and now Valerie's.

When he finally turned away from the bracket, he found Valerie, Maya, and Gianna bustling around in the kitchen, setting up the food for self-serving on the countertops. The scent of refried beans, rice, and various meats made his stomach growl embarrassingly.

"Sit."

He heard the sharp command moments before he and Maya were pushed towards the breakfast bar.

"Just let me—" Maya began to protest.

"Sit," Gianna repeated, pointing to the chairs. "You've been up cooking all of this food for who knows how long. And you were practically melting in the sun while working on the fence. Everything's done now. You can eat before more people get here."

"No point in arguing with her when she gets like this," Valerie said with a grin as she placed two ice filled glasses of water in front of Hunter and Maya after they sat. "She'll fix you a plate next."

Curious to see if she would follow through, Hunter

looked at Gianna. She wore a light blue romper dotted with loud orange palm leaves with sleeves that fluttered around her shoulders. It was the kind of thing someone wore when they didn't care about being noticed, which was very much on brand for Gianna. He let his eyes drift, just for a second, over the subtle rise of her chest before snapping them lower, tracing the shape of the fabric as it cinched at her waist and then loosened again, ending in shorts that skimmed just above her knees.

It meant nothing. He wasn't looking, not really. Just taking in his surroundings. Like anyone would.

But then she turned to reach for something and the fabric shifted just enough to show the curve of her ass. Not much. Just enough. He looked away so fast his neck tensed.

Fuck. What was wrong with him?

He rubbed the back of his neck, suddenly too warm, trying to blink the image out of his head. He exhaled through his nose, jaw tight and lifted his glass to take another sip of water. Beside him, Maya pouted, clearly put out.

"I just wanted to go get that game for you," she whined.

Gianna began filling two plates with food. "You can get it later."

"I'll forget later," she complained.

"Isn't Ruben still home?" Valerie asked. She placed an open beer in front of Hunter. "Have him bring it over."

"Thanks," he murmured, still distracted.

"He won't be able to find where I hid it. Ooh, thank you," she said to Valerie, taking the glass of wine gratefully.

"So set a reminder on your watch." Gianna set a plate in front of Hunter and Maya, both piled with rice, beans, and meat. "Or go get it after you eat."

Moments later, Valerie brought over a bowl of tortilla chips and a plate of tortillas, with Gianna following close behind her with bowls full of salsa, sour cream, and limes. They returned to the kitchen to make their own plates.

"Why are you hiding a game anyway?" Valerie asked.

"Is this the game you were trying to give me?" Hunter asked, finally feeling sane again.

"Yeah," Maya said, answering Hunter's question first. "My brother gave the boys a game I think they're too young to play. Gianna and Hunter are the only gamers I know so I figured one of them would want it. Hunter already has it so I need you to take it off my hands."

Curious, Gianna joined them at the counter and set her plate down before pulling her phone out of her pocket. "What's the game called?"

Hunter shifted uncomfortably in the chair, grateful that she spoke before he could ask if she was really a gamer. Something that would have been incredibly stupid and misogynistic to ask. Why was that even his first thought? Dumb habits were harder to break than he realized. Gianna leaned on her elbows on the counter beside him and opened up her PlayStation App, giving him a view of what she was doing.

"Vault Hunter 2," he said finally. He looked over her screen, surprised to discover that they played many of the same games.

"Sounds familiar," she mumbled, her attention focused on reading about the game now that she found it. "I think I saw an ad about it a few months ago."

"The third one was released earlier this summer. I haven't played it yet as it's had mixed reviews. Better game play and graphics than the second, but shit story in comparison."

"RPG, FPS. Online *and* couch co-op," she added, surprised by the latter. "Now I'm really interested."

Maya blinked at her. "Is that some sort of coder's language?"

"No." Hunter grinned. "I could tell you what she means but you probably still wouldn't get it."

"Or care," Gianna said with a smirk. "Are you playing it right now?"

"Not anymore. It's not as fun playing by yourself and it's hard to find someone to play with because most people are playing Death Divers now."

"Put in your gamertag. Let's try it this weekend," she said, sliding her phone over to him. "I'm getting bored with Death Divers, so it will be nice to play something different."

He felt some of his tension return when he picked up her phone. As he put in his information, he couldn't stop the unwanted thought that this was just some sort of ruse to flirt with him. For a moment earlier he thought that he caught her checking him out. Turns out, she just wanted his business card. So why did he still assume that she had ulterior motives?

Rolling his shoulder in annoyance, he slid the phone back to Gianna, before vacating the chair. He needed some space before he actually said some of his stupid thoughts out loud.

"Here, sit and eat. I'll save the rest for later."

Gianna sat and happily started filling a tortilla. "Sorry. Decided to err on the side of caution and just put everything on the plate since I don't know exactly what you two prefer."

"I appreciate it," he said honestly and put his plate in the microwave just as the doorbell rang. "I'll get it, you ladies finish up."

Grateful for the task, he made his escape, relaxing a little as he approached the door. Still, his pulse was doing that annoying thing in his throat. The one that usually came with bad decisions and worse timing.

He knew it was stupid to avoid her. That in itself was likely a bad decision. But Gianna was trouble and she flustered him more than he cared to admit. Until he could figure out exactly why she made his pulse jump and his thoughts scatter, he would do well to keep his distance.

CHAPTER 4

The Halls and the Kobayashis knew how to throw a party. Gianna was a little bit sad that she had missed out on their 4th of July party that year. Since her monthly dinner tradition with her sister happened to fall on the 4th this year, she had celebrated the holiday with her family instead and missed out on what she assumed had been just as entertaining as this party.

Not that she hadn't thoroughly enjoyed her own family, but this type of party was her ideal environment. There were so many people to talk to, plenty of food and beverage to enjoy, and entertainment in the form of games.

Valerie's optional bracket games ranged in difficulty from simple to a tad bit hard core. The first round of games included as many people as possible in a game of 90's musical chairs. Thanks to the new backyard configuration, quite a few people had been able to join. Despite the heat, they all circled around the chairs, singing and dancing to snippets of the 90's most popular hits. Half the people were outed just because they had been too distracted enjoying the music to pay any real attention to the game.

Of course, that meant that the only ones that actually moved on to the next bracket were all of the truly competitive people. Once back inside the soothing embrace of the air conditioning, the party split between those who wanted to eat and watch and those who wanted the silly trophy Valerie had ordered online.

In between games, Gianna stuffed herself on Maya's delicious food or wandered from person to person, catching up or delving into brief, but deep conversations.

After the second game, she managed to get some face time with London, Tony, and Hunter, though Hunter was pulled into his own game before they could really talk. However, it gave her an opportunity to assess how things were between her best friend and her man. Fortunately, they both looked a little less haunted and a lot happier than they had been on Thursday. It would take some time, but she could see that the bridge between them was well on the mend.

She was, much to her annoyance, defeated by Hunter's younger brother in flip cup, of all things. She spent a bit of time talking to him and his boyfriend while the remaining competitors finished their round of the game. James Hall had the devastating, Usher level good looks like the rest of the Hall men. Unlike his brother however, James was friendly, quick to laugh, and as talkative as she was. It was hard to believe that they were even brothers.

Gianna searched the room for Hunter, realizing that she hadn't had much of an opportunity to talk to him, despite her best efforts to do so. By the time she realized it and made a concerted effort to try to talk to him, she began to suspect that it wasn't by chance.

She leaned against the kitchen island, beer in hand, and let her gaze rest on Hunter. He was in the middle of a flip cup game with Tony, bent slightly forward in concentration, his focus sharp but easy. His skin had a low, golden sheen under the overhead light, and his short fade was sharp enough to make her fingertips itch.

"Ayy!" He shouted after he flipped another cup, his grin wide and cocky.

Her pulse skittered in response. *Gianna, you in danger girl,* she thought to herself.

She took a slow sip of beer, the taste bitter, but it gave her something to do with her mouth while she watched. Every move he made was smooth. Shoulders rolling when he laughed, fingers tapping the table in rhythm, his voice deep and relaxed when he called out playful trash talk.

The crowd dispersed after the game ended, but Hunter and Tony remained to clean up so Jun could force Valerie to take a minute to sit and relax. Gianna stayed where she was, her eyes drifting back to him again. Drawn by heat, gravity, and something else she wasn't ready to name.

Who was this man who laughed and grinned so easily with others, but couldn't seem to spare her a casual glance? Why did she so desperately crave the same thing he gave so freely to others when she suspected he didn't even like her? She was clearly becoming a masochist, and it deeply annoyed her. He wasn't *that* good looking.

But even still, she wanted to repair their relationship. She was just clouding her intentions a little by allowing the nostalgia of her brief high school crush on him to influence how she felt about him today.

She knew that London and Hunter had grown close during their time at UCLA, but she knew very little about their friendship after they graduated. The chummy way Tony and Hunter chatted made it obvious that this wasn't their first time meeting, so it was safe to assume that London's friendship with Hunter hadn't changed much.

Valerie also hadn't mentioned him very often, if at all, since relocating from San Diego, but clearly their relationship hadn't changed either.

She felt a spark of guilt and shame for not keeping in touch with him after he finished tutoring her before she reminded herself that her life had become exceptionally difficult the minute she hit her junior year in high school. She hadn't been in the right emotional or mental space to maintain any more relationships outside of the ones she had with her two besties, her sister, and her aunt.

And, if she recalled correctly, hadn't Hunter all but disappeared his senior year? There had been no effort on his part to maintain their friendship either so she wasn't the only guilty party.

"Next round starts in five minutes," Jun yelled from the living room, jarring her from her thoughts.

Tony and Hunter didn't hear him, so she pushed from the counter to go tell them. Tony's back was to her, but Hunter was leaning against the table facing the kitchen. Their eyes met briefly as she approached, but his quickly looked away as he stood. Did he tense up when he had been so relaxed as he conversed with Tony these last ten minutes?

"Hey, you two," Gianna said, smiling while her thoughts whirled in confusion.

Tony turned and greeted her warmly, even knowing she was planning to kick his ass. "Hey, Gianna."

"Jun says the next round will start in five minutes. Tony, why don't you keep me company since the Halls kicked both our asses?"

Tony laughed. "I'm told they have an unfair advantage since they grew up having these competitions. I don't think we stood a chance."

She looked up at Hunter and grinned. "I never would have imagined that the Halls were playing flip cup in elementary school."

"Obviously, we weren't playi—"

"Obviously," she said, cutting him off. "I was just joking."

"Don't let him off the hook," Tony interjected. "I'm not convinced Ruben, James, and Hunter hadn't developed and honed those flipping skills long before college."

"You may be right," she said thoughtfully, looking to Hunter again to confirm.

He only shrugged in response, baffling her. His refusal to talk only added more confirmation to her suspicion. She gave him one more chance.

"What's the next game?" she asked, meeting his eyes.

"Not sure," he said.

Gianna waited a beat before speaking, but she still couldn't keep the annoyance out of her voice. "Is it my imagination or do you refuse to say more than three words to me?"

Caught, Hunter simply stared at her. Before he could figure out how to respond, he was saved when London arrived with reinforcements.

"There you are!" Maya exclaimed. She pushed

Gianna toward the back door. "Let's go get that game before I forget. Again."

"Hunter," London said, slipping her arm through his arm to pull him through the kitchen. "I brought Maya over here because I thought Tony needed to be rescued from Gianna, not you."

"And I appreciate it," Tony said, following behind her. "But she definitely is on to you, Hunter."

Hunter clenched his jaw. "I don't know what you're talking about."

London stopped to look at him before releasing his arm to smile sweetly at Tony. "Hey, babe. Can you tell me what I missed?"

He actually wanted to gasp. "That's just low, London. He's still kissing your ass."

"He pretty much clammed up the minute she came over," Tony confessed with a grin and no shame whatsoever. "Takes me back to… Well, I really don't want to make any assumptions so I won't say more. She called him out on it right before you came over."

"Takes you back to what?" London demanded. Then she turned to Hunter. She would question Tony later. "Why won't you talk to her? Didn't I warn you that you're inviting the wrong kind of attention by throwing up a wall between you two? She just wants to be your friend."

"I really don't understand why either of you are making a big deal about me not having much to say to her. I hardly know her."

London shook her head. "Wow. Now I know how stupid I sounded at Valerie's wedding. It's no wonder Gianna snapped at me."

"What are you talking about?"

"It's time for the semi-final round!" Jun declared.

"Ruben, James, Hunter, and Alena. Please come choose your drivers. First and second place will advance to the finals."

"You definitely fucked up and I'm not about to get in the way of you finding out. Good luck."

Hunter watched London storm off into the living room, Tony on her heels. Baffled and annoyed, he forced himself to set the whole thing aside as he got into the game. They were going to play Mario Kart Double Dash. If this was Ruben's Game Cube, then he was in for a challenge. It was the only game that Ruben ever played, and he was pretty sure he still played it to this day.

Hunter managed to take second place. Poor Alena hadn't known what she was doing at all while James used every race to purposefully wreak havoc on Hunter and Ruben. He might have been able to take first, but his focus kept slipping back to Gianna's question. To London's ominous words.

As a result, Ruben absolutely obliterated him in Super Smash Bros, winning the tournament. Luckily, the party had thinned out so he was spared from massive embarrassment. He could hear some people in the kitchen packing up food and cleaning. He tried to use the embarrassing loss as an excuse to leave.

"Not yet! Please eat some desert," Valerie begged as she ran in from the kitchen. "Or at least take some home with you."

"Alright," he said, going to the kitchen to fill his plate.

"Cake and ice cream incoming," Tony announced as he walked into the living room with two plates in his hand.

He handed a plate to Gianna, who had wandered

back in just in time to see Hunter get destroyed.

"Ooh, I could get use to this kind of service. Thanks."

"Anything to stay on your good side," he shared, sitting on the other couch next to London.

She narrowed her eyes at Tony. "Anything?"

"Uhm…."

London laughed. "She's not going to torture you. Pretty sure she means money."

He looked at her. "Money?"

"For the scholarship fund you're starting, right?" Jun said around a piece of cake as he walked in the living room. "I talked to Dustin about it before he left. He loves the idea so we're in."

"Oh? Tell me more," Tony said, interest evident in his face.

"I run a non-profit called Count Her In." She resisted the urge to glance where Hunter sat at the kitchen counter. "I provide free math tutoring to middle through high school, and occasionally college, girls and young women."

"That's pretty cool," Tony said, impressed.

"Thanks," she said, checking the need to squirm. Her non-profit wasn't a secret, but she only just started brainstorming this idea so it was weird sharing it with so many people so soon. "A girl I tutored a few years ago expressed interest in pursuing something in STEM and her mom reached out to me to find out if I knew of any STEM specific scholarships. There are a few, but I got this idea of offering scholarships through Count Her In to add to that list. I'm thinking something around five thousand a year, but obviously that will depend on how much money I can pool together and how many scholarships I award. I'm still working out the details."

"Which I will help you with," London shared, leaning forward. "And I'm already making a mental list of lawyers that I can send your way."

"I can offer potential donors for that list," Tony added. "That's even better than the free tutoring."

Gianna shrugged. "It's just necessary. Women are still, unfortunately, underrepresented in STEM, and usually just because girls are still being told they can't be good at math just because they're girls. I know that's why I was terrible at it."

"No shit?" Jun asked in surprise. "I just assumed you've always been good at it."

"Not even," she chuckled, wondering if anyone saw the stare that she felt boring through her soul. She thought it came from Hunter, but was still to annoyed with him to confirm. "I struggled from elementary through high school. I had a tutor and that changed literally everything for me. I fell in love with math and now I'm just trying to pay it forward."

Hunter pushed away from the counter to throw his plate away. He should say something, but he just couldn't figure out the words. His silence would tell Gianna and London that he was in fact avoiding speaking to Gianna, but he really didn't have anything to say this time around.

He didn't know anything about this Gianna, and it was stupid of him to treat her like they were still in high school.

Embarrassed, he silently helped gather chairs and put furniture back in its place. The women packed up the rest of the food, leaving leftovers for those who wanted them for tomorrow, and took the rest over to Maya's house so she could drop it off at the homeless shelter.

When Gianna came back, only Tony, Ruben, and Jun were in the living room. Grateful that she didn't have to see Hunter, she approached them to say her goodbyes.

Jun stood to hug her. "Drive safe, gorgeous. You've got a long drive."

"Thanks, Jun." She turned to Tony who had stood as well. "London looks happier today."

"We're definitely doing better," he said, his embarrassment evident. "I just want her to be happy."

"You'll get there. In the meantime…"

It gave her an inappropriate amount of pleasure to see the surprise fill his eyes when she socked him in the stomach. Since he was mending things and London was clearly happier, she pulled the punch and only hit him hard enough to knock a little wind out of him.

She wasn't expecting, however, the hard press of the body against her back or the thick arms that locked around hers. There was a split second of panic, of fear, before her training kicked in. She lifted her arms as she widened and slightly dropped her stance. Then she thrust her butt into her attacker's belly. His grip immediately loosened when he was pushed backward. She was turning, her arms coming up in defense, when she heard her own internal voice telling her to calm down. Telling her she was safe.

She was safe.

When she looked down, she saw that it was Hunter who sat on his ass, his face full of rage as he struggled to breathe. Behind her, Ruben and Jun roared with laughter. Even Tony, who had just barely caught his breath, wheezed out a laugh.

Worried the nerves would show, she knelt beside

Hunter to rub his back and willed her own anger to take over.

"You'd breathe better if you'd stop laughing at the poor guy," she said, scowling at Tony. "Hunter, you need to sit upright. There you go. Now breathe in slowly through your mouth while pushing your stomach out, and then suck your stomach back in as your exhale to stretch out your diaphragm."

Hunter slanted her a dirty look. Did she really just knock the wind out of him and turn right around to nurse him back to health? And did she have to touch him? She was just making it worse.

"There you go," she repeated.

Tony wiped tears from his eyes and sucked in a breath before blowing it out. "Honestly, I was expecting what he got."

Gianna stood and glared at him. "If you ever hurt my friend again, I'll do much worse."

"Yeah, got the message, loud and clear. We good?"

"Oh, my god. What happened?" London demanded, as she came inside.

Hunter picked himself up from the ground and glared at Gianna. "Your friend is out here attacking people. She just sucker punched your boyfriend."

London looked over at Gianna, who was grinning and putting her arms around Tony's waist. This seemed to amuse Tony who grinned and tossed his arm around her shoulder in response.

"We had an agreement. A contract if you will," Gianna explained.

"You know how I feel about agreements, London," he said darkly, his eyes basically undressing her.

"Oh, gross," Gianna laughed and pushed Tony toward London.

"If I fuck up again, I'll bring my own body bag. Deal?"

Gianna smiled at him. "You won't fuck up again."

"Never again," he promised, taking London's hand and pulling her to him.

"So, everyone is just okay with Gianna attacking people?" Hunter demanded.

"Well, like I said, we had an agreement so it wasn't like that," Gianna explained, glaring at him. "You attacked me. Grabbed me from behind. I defended myself. You don't like the consequences? Then keep your hands to yourself."

He gaped at her as she calmly walked away, then whipped around in shock when London slapped his arm.

"You attacked her from behind?"

"To stop her from beating up your boyfriend! Why are you mad at me?"

She glared at him. "When we were in college, what did you tell me do if someone, anyone grabbed me?"

He started to speak and then shut his mouth.

"Yeah, that's what I thought," she said, shaking her head, and then went to Gianna.

Something passed between them, some unspoken girl language that he had seen time and time again between his own sisters but had no way of deciphering. Gianna's smile wobbled for the briefest moment before she forced it back in place and shook her head. She squeezed London's hand before easing away to put her shoes on. He was the only one who saw it since everyone else was still laughing at him.

"Bye everyone!" She called, and went out the front door with London.

Jun passed him a beer. "Embarrassing, but could

have been worse. She pulled that punch and definitely stopped herself from going full on black belt on you."

"Working on her second degree." Tony shared. "Appreciate you coming to my defense, though. Unlike these so-called friends"

"It's not my fault that you two aren't bright enough not to piss off a black belt," Jun pointed out.

Ruben chuckled. "Second degree black belt. She passed last month."

"I'm knocking that damn fence down. No," he said darkly. "I'm putting the old shit back up."

Having had enough embarrassment for the day, he stormed off, desperate to be anywhere but here.

CHAPTER 5

Inside his two-bedroom house, Hunter kicked off his shoes and stalked to his room to toss his bag by the door and strip. Since he'd forgotten to turn on the AC unit, the house was like a sauna so he plopped himself on the dark grey couch wearing only boxers until it cooled down.

His place wasn't anything fancy like Jun and Valerie's. There were a lot of things he planned to do to make it fancy, but those things hadn't happened yet. He looked around while his PS5 loaded. The coffee and dining table he and his brother built still needed to be stained. A few weekends ago, he finally installed the kitchen cabinet doors after months of sitting in his garage after he resurfaced and painted them. His sister was itching to get over here to replace the backsplash, but their schedules hadn't aligned just yet.

It was easy to assume that time was limitless, but he knew better.

The system notified him of a friend request, and he was forced to think of Gianna again. He had driven home with the radio on full blast as a distraction. Despite that, his mind played back the last hour of the night on repeat. He could see Gianna, looking oddly timid, as she told the story of her business. Count Her

In, she called it.

He had looked it up in the dark, quiet of his car before he left.

It was hard to believe that he had made such a tremendous impact on her life. The knowledge left him feeling a jumble of emotions, each tripping over the other before he could give it a name. He tried to unwind the tangled mess, but he just kept seeing her sitting on that couch, confessing that she loved math. Because of him.

Math had always come easily and naturally to him. He had loved the complex order of numbers for as long as he could remember. His parents had nurtured it through construction and supported him in getting access to advanced classes in middle and high school.

He fell into tutoring accidently the summer before his sophomore year. As he often did during his school breaks, he worked for Hall Construction. While on a job, he had garnered the attention of the client's son who had been more than a little jealous that a kid so close in his age was allowed to use power tools without supervision.

Todd Wellington IV had been born into a world of generational wealth. His father, and the father before him, were wealthy career politicians whose footsteps he had no intention of following. At the age of fifteen, his focus was only on girls, booze, and spending his father's money until he saw Hunter on the circular saw.

Used to getting his way, Todd didn't think twice about ordering the crew to teach him. When Hunter's dad refused and forbade his team from doing that, Todd went to his own father. Much to Todd's dismay, Wellington III wasn't on his side, reminding Todd that his failed courses in math would prevent him from understanding anything the crew was doing.

Todd's solution to that problem was to corner Hunter one afternoon and demand he tutor him. In the end, Hunter was paid to tutor and train Todd as it was the first and last time that Todd took an independent interest anything constructive.

While Hunter wouldn't claim that he had changed Todd's life for the better, the experience did change his own. Tutoring became something he enjoyed almost as much as building and it helped him get over some of his social anxiety. He tutored several more kids after Todd and thought he had been managing his anxiety well until he started tutoring Gianna.

She hadn't been the only girl to trip him up back then, but she had been the only constant because of her friendship with his cousin. The kind, beautiful, live wire who talked almost as much as she listened. She was always friendly to him, and that friendship was a constant torture to him.

It irritated him that merely being in her presence again tripped him up so much, just as it had in high school. He felt completely out of character whenever her talked to her. First, the disastrous scene in Hawaii and now the even more catastrophic ending at tonight's party.

Worse still, he couldn't deny that on both occasions, he had felt… something. A flicker. A pull. Something low and insistent that curled in his gut before he could shut it down. He told himself it was nothing. Just a reaction. A glitch in his otherwise well-ordered system. But deep down, in the quiet spaces he didn't like to acknowledge, he knew better. There was something about her that got under his skin. And for reasons he couldn't explain or control, that reality had started to stick.

He hated that. Hated how aware he was of her when she entered a room. Hated how his mind wandered back to the curve of her smile or the challenge in her eyes. Hated most of all that no matter how many excuses he gave himself, none of them held up under the weight of her presence.

Whatever it was he felt, it was there. And it was growing. Quietly. Relentlessly. Against his better judgment.

His thoughts drifted back to when he grabbed her. She had fit so snug in arms, had been soft and warm, before striking him like a battering ram. When she had rubbed his back, both her tone and her touch had been so gentle, her eyes so kind. Then everything about her had been hard and cold when she accused him of attacking her. The combination of such opposites was fascinating.

He was impressed with how she handled herself. With how she defended London. Hunter had become very protective over London in college. They had spent three years together at the University of California, Los Angeles where he obtained his Masters of Arts in Architecture & Urban Design. It had been comforting to have someone from home around during those years, especially as he broke out of the shy shell that had made his high school years miserable.

London had tried, more than once, to understand why he bristled every time her best friend's name came up, but his answers had always fallen flat. The truth was, he hadn't fully understood it himself. It wasn't until years later, sitting across from a therapist, that he began to untangle the knot.

His feelings for Gianna had been too layered, too

volatile to explain in simple terms. Desire blurred with resentment, admiration tainted by a sharp edge of inadequacy. What unsettled him most was how those emotions hadn't stayed contained. They had festered, spread, and eventually hardened into something uglier.

It wasn't easy to admit how much of his cynicism toward women had begun with Gianna, and the way she had made him feel both seen and dismissed in the same breath. That contradiction had gnawed at him until the only way he knew how to cope was to shift blame, to frame women as the problem instead of confronting his own wounds. His complicated feelings toward her hadn't just lingered. They had cracked something open in him, a gateway into the bitter, hollow allure of misogyny.

In college, it was depressingly easy to find men with like minds. At the gym, in classes, at sporting events. The more social he became, the more solidified the misogynistic echo chamber became. As he and his friends pursued and dated women, they found more and more to shout into the void. It didn't get any better after graduating. The world of constructure became an even bigger breeding ground for that toxic thinking.

Without therapy, he knew he might have slipped right back into that world the moment he saw her again. Because Gianna hadn't grown into some stranger, she'd grown into someone frustratingly familiar. They had a lot in common now. A love of math, the responsibility of running a nonprofit, even a streak of competitiveness that once drew them together and now felt like dangerous kindling. As he scrolled her profile, noticing the games she played and realizing how many of them overlapped with his own, it should have been enough to spark the beginnings of a friendship. Maybe even a second chance.

But it didn't. Instead, it left him uneasy, tightening his chest with the same old contradiction. Drawn to her, yet wary of what she stirred up inside him. The rational part of him knew there was common ground for something good. The other part, the part that remembered what she had once awakened in him, whispered that the safest course of action was to turn and run the other way.

He had a lot to fucking unpack and not only did he have no clue where to start. Thankfully, his next therapy appointment was in a few weeks. Until then, he had to figure out if he could accept her being in his life as easily as he accepted her friend request.

∞∞∞∞∞∞

Hunter pulled up to the job site after a painful hour stuck in traffic. A fender bender on HWY 50 off Watt Avenue had him crawling along for forty-five minutes on his way from Rancho Cordova to East Sacramento. After making it through that, he hit the usual back up on the Business 80 Loop. Now he had a headache that would likely morph into a full-blown migraine by lunch time.

Even still, he loved his job. Not everyone had the pleasure of doing the work they loved, and fortunately for him, he liked the job that he had been raised to do.

Hall Construction had been started by his grandfather, Benjamin Hall I, in the late 1950s. His father, Benjamin Hall II, was currently at the helm. It had always been an unspoken expectation that

Benjamin Hunter Hall III would take over the family business.

Although Hunter had no desire to run Hall Construction, his intention had been to suck it up and do so until that fateful accident fifteen months ago. Since then, he had taken a hard look at his life and knew he wanted to change some things.

Construction work already took up quite a bit of his time and energy, and some of that was an accidental personal choice. It was his friend, his lover, and confidant. When he didn't have many people from those categories to check on or care for him after the accident, it was a hard reality to reconcile. Family he had in abundance. But when he was sitting alone in the quiet of his home, he wanted somebody there who loved him not because of the blood they shared.

Taking over the family business would only interfere with him finding someone to be there.

Running Hall Construction just wasn't for him. Not in the way that his father wanted. After months of arguing, it was his sister, Madison, who had put an end to the entire thing when she declared that she would be taking over the family business.

Hunter grinned at the memory. His father had been blindsided, but Madison laid it all out. It was her, after all, who had gone to school for business administration.

And as the construction manager who coordinated and supervised all of their projects, she already had her finger on the pulse of everything that was Hall Construction. Hunter, on the other hand, focused more on the architecture and civil engineering of a project or on the non-profit.

Madison was the only choice and she happily pulled

her father's head out of his own ass so he could see it.

Firmly put in their place, it didn't take long for him and his father to fall in line. Hunter took on more responsibilities as the construction manager while his dad spent the next three months handing the business over to his first-born daughter instead of his first-born son. Everyone was happy with the arrangement now.

If only the rest of his life could fall so neatly into place.

After the tragic car accident that had cost other's their lives but spared his, he decided that he wanted to live life, not just experience it. He wanted to spend more time enjoying his family and friends. He wanted to find someone he could start a serious relationship with that might one day lead to the love that his parents had.

So far, all he had managed to accomplish was spending more time with his extended family. That's why he went to Valerie's wedding, and her Labor Day party. He now saw more of his uncle's children than he had in years, even though they all lived in Sacramento all his life.

He still didn't get out with friends as often as he liked, and that was mostly because he didn't have many outside of the construction world. After spending hours with them at a job site, he rarely had the desire to spend even more time with them outside of work.

Tapping his fingers on his steering wheel as he finally took the exit off the freeway, he again considered getting on one of those dating apps. It was something that might be worth trying at least once, and while it wasn't how he imagined he would find a partner, he acknowledged that it was a fairly common way for many people to find love these days.

Despite the traffic, he still arrived a few minutes before his crew. He left early to get coffee and donuts, but unfortunately that plan didn't pan out. Instead, he would have to settle for the protein bar he pulled from his glove compartment for breakfast. After removing the wrapper, he shoved it in his mouth and pushed out of his truck.

His crew was split between two job sites this month. He would start his day at the first site where they were doing a complete gut job of the first floor. They would eventually put in a new kitchen, a half bath, and flooring. His younger brother James, who was their electrician, had finished all of the electrical upgrades including installing new pot lights on Thursday. His younger sister Naomi, who was finishing the last year of her plumbing apprenticeship, had worked with her mentor, Brian on all of the plumbing as well.

The inspector came midday Friday, clearing them to close everything up with drywall. They had used the rest of that day to put in the insulation and saved the drywall so they could knock out the job in one day. Most of the work was done at the other job site, and that meant more people were available for today. His plan was to have drywall up so the house would be ready for the painters tomorrow.

He didn't wait much longer for his crew to show. Soon after, Hunter laid out the plan for the day, but didn't outright assign people to specific tasks. Most of the crew had worked for Hall Construction for years and since this was a fairly straight forward job, there was a natural flow to their teamwork that didn't necessitate a strict approach. Most of his job was addressing any problems that arose naturally or ones created by their own mistakes. The other large part was keeping them from getting too distracted so they could stay on schedule.

Sometimes, like today, he worked too, and within the hour, work was in full swing and his team slid in to their usual shit talking banter.

"I wish you could have been there," Eddie said as he screwed in the piece of drywall Hunter had just brought in. "The man got shit faced and still thought the women would come flocking."

Even though he missed the first part of the conversation, Hunter could guess who he was talking about. "Where did you all end up going?"

"Darling Aviary. It's right across from DOCO."

"Never heard of it," Hunter confessed.

Eddie shook his head. "And that's why we always ask you to hang with us! You don't get out enough."

"All he missed was Todd striking out," Jose said as he carried in another drywall sheet. "Drinking more, and then striking out again. On repeat until he was completely trashed."

"Thursday is a shit night to go out. I told you that," Todd said in defense as he hefted in a bucket of joint compound. "We should have waited until Friday."

Jose chuckled. "So, you only got game on the weekend?"

"I got game on any day that ends with Y," Todd declared.

"Are you still hung up on that brunette?" Eddie paused to ask. "Red vest and red shoes, looking like she came straight from a board meeting and who obviously wanted absolutely nothing to do with him?"

"That's the one," Jose declared.

Eddie whistled, bringing her back to his mind. "Yeah, she was pretty hot."

"Like a goddess," Pablo said, finally joining in on the conversation. "You can't pull a woman like her with your rich frat boy act."

"It's not an act," Jose said with a grin. "He still thinks he's a rich."

"Fuck you," Todd said, his face darkening with anger.

"Don't get mad, man. You just gotta get better at recognizing when a woman is out of your league," Pablo encouraged.

Hunter snorted. Todd still thought everyone, especially women, were out of *his* league.

"You say that because you can only pull low value women. A high value man like myself? We only want the best and any woman worth being with us is going to play a little hard to get."

Jose laughed. "How you going to play the game if you don't even have her name or number?"

Todd shrugged it off, even though deep down, he was pissed that the brunette had shot him down. "Just means the bitch was low value after all."

"Knock it off, Todd. You don't have any right to talk about her like that. She's not obligated to be interested in you just because you were interested in her," Hunter said harshly. Then, because he did feel a little bad for his friend, he added, "You're all shitting on Todd instead of bragging about your own pull, so I guess that means you all struck out."

"I was just there to drink. I already got a girl," Pablo reminded him.

"Didn't she dump your ass last week?" Eddie asked.

Hunter shook his head as he went back to the garage for more drywall. Not too long ago, he would have joined in on the conversation, but ever since he started therapy, he made a conscious effort to reign in the negativity he spewed about the opposite sex. And although it wasn't always easy, he tried to get his crew to do the same. In the end, it seemed like men were only good at talking shit, whether it was about women or each other.

Jose and Todd were by far the worst at this, though their targets were different. Jose never really liked Todd and he jumped on any opportunity to kick the man if he was down. Unfortunately for Todd, down seemed to be his new normal.

Despite the tutoring and his interest in construction, Todd couldn't be more than what he was nurtured to be his whole life. And so, the spoiled little rich kid who was used to throwing around money and always getting his way had convinced his father to buy him a construction company. For five years, his father kept the business afloat and put out the constant fires created by Todd as a result of him chasing after clients, their wives, or their daughters.

Eventually, he had an affair with the wrong woman. Her husband went to Todd's father, told him of his deeds, bought the company himself and fired Todd.

But karma wasn't done there. After Todd went whining to his father, he learned that not only would his father not bail him out again, but that he had also cut him out of his will and stripped him of his inheritance.

He survived six months before he came crawling to Hunter to beg for a job. At the time, Hunter was still recovering from a messy break up and it was because of their shared vitriol for women that they reconnected. Because of course Todd's predicament was not a direct result of his own behavior, but because the woman he had seduced had gotten them caught. It was always the woman's fault in Todd's world.

Hunter was still embarrassed that he and Todd had ever seen eye to eye on women. In the two years that Todd had worked for Hall Construction, Hunter knew that his opinions hadn't changed at all. His own change started to happen slowly, but the lonely wakeup call after the accident put him on a fast track to be better. He went all out to ensure that he didn't still harbor those same sexist thoughts. Of course he had more growing to do, but he liked to believe that he was getting better by the day.

The fact that Todd wasn't the only one who messed up with a beautiful brunette this weekend made it even more obvious that he still had room to improve. He could prove to himself, and to Gianna, that he was better by making amends. He paused for a moment, setting the drywall sheet against the wall to remove his phone from his pocket. Opening up his PlayStation app, he stared at Gianna's handle for a moment, wondering what he could say to explain away his behavior.

He sent her a message to see if she would be open to trying Vault Hunter 2 with him on Friday. That gave him plenty of time to think about what he could say to her.

When the work day was done and he was finally home, Hunter took a much-needed shower before reheating the Chinese food he had stopped to pick up. It had been a long week, and the weekend had proven to be even longer. Next week would be just as busy so he wanted to spend the last hours of this day doing as little as possible.

He sat on his faded, gray couch and watched a

movie. When that was over, he went online to game and played until it was well past time to call it a night. Despite accepting Gianna's friendship request, she hadn't come online yet, much to his relief.

He still hadn't figured out what to tell her. What would he say? *You made me feel like I was in high school again, so I avoided you.* Even in his head he knew he sounded like a childish dumbass. He would need to learn how to deal with whatever it was sooner rather than later. Whether he liked it or not, he was going to have to coexist with Gianna. She was fundamental in London and Valerie's lives and since he wanted to be in theirs, he had to get used to Gianna as well.

CHAPTER 6

"So, you want to tell me why you were avoiding me at Valerie's?"

"Damn," Hunter managed after a moment of silence. "Straight to the point."

Through his headphones, he heard Gianna chuckle and shift around like she was getting into a more comfortable position.

"I learned a long time ago that it's better to clear things up to avoid misunderstandings. What gives, Hunter? I know we haven't talked since high school, but we were always friendly."

The mention of high school and her brand of *friendly* made him feel a little of that sexist rage that he had come to recognize. Had high school really been that simple for her? He could, by her suggestion, clear things up, but he wasn't ready to delve into that yet, especially with her.

"Honestly, seeing you again took me back to high school," he said with a sigh. "I hated high school."

"Say less," she said, her voice full of sympathy. "I don't like dwelling on my time in high school either. But you see Valerie and London all the time. Is it the same with them?"

"No. It's different. Valerie is my cousin so we were always together outside of high school and I went to college with London."

"And you've only known me from high school. I wonder which version of me lives in your head," she mumbled.

"What does that mean?"

"Nothing. Tell me about the person you are today while this update installs."

"What do you want to know?" He asked, happy to change the subject, and started the game. Though he would be lying if he said he didn't want to know why she hated high school too.

"What have you been up to all these years? I know that you and London have always been friends, but I feel like she's talked about you more often in the last few months"

"Honestly, just work. I've been trying to spend more time with family to change that."

"I get that. What made you want to change?"

It was easier to talk about it now, but he still didn't like to. Because he didn't, he forced himself to tell her.

"A big rig plowed through traffic on 99 and caused a huge accident. Nearly fifteen cars. Some people didn't survive it. I did, so I figured I better make the most of the life that had been spared and actually start living it instead of only working."

"Damn. I'm sorry, Hunter. I didn't mean to—"

"It's fine. It's been almost eighteen months since it happened."

"Well, I'm glad you're okay," she replied genuinely before quickly changing the subject. "At Valerie's party, James mentioned that you all work together. How many siblings do you have? Do they all work with you?"

"Hall Construction is a family business. My parents run it, or rather they did. They just retired. Madison, my younger sister, runs the business itself now and I'm the construction manager. The twins, James and Naomi, have their own roles."

"Oh, I didn't know James has a twin!"

"Yep. Twins run in the Hall family. My grandfather had a twin."

"Cool."

"What about your family?"

"It's just me and my older sister, Emilia, my sister-in-law, and their daughter. Small by comparison."

"Still a family. You're close to your sister I guess?"

"Absolutely. Update is done. Let's play!" While it loaded, she kept the conversation going. "When did you start playing video games?"

"Pretty sure I always did. Started with basketball and football games. Figured since I lacked the coordination to play it in real life, I could stay in the loop by watching games or playing video games. Then I just started taking recommendations from people or trying things that looked interesting."

"You don't play many sports games anymore. We pretty much have the same game play history. Why did you switch?"

"I guess online gaming took over, and RPGs are better suited for it, I think. What about you? How did you get your start?"

She didn't respond right away, caught up, he was sure, in deciding which character to choose. He hoped she would answer because he was actually really curious about it. Female gamers weren't as rare as they once had been, but the gaming world was still pretty toxic toward them.

"Dance Dance Revolution," she said after a while.

He laughed. "Is it weird that I can actually picture you playing that? How old were you when that game came out?"

"Well, I discovered it at our high school grad night at Golf Land so it probably came out a few years before that in order to make it into the arcade. Did you go to yours?"

"Yeah," he said, recalling the all-night party the amusement park hosted for graduating seniors. "But I don't think it was there when I went."

"Well, I played it so much that night that when I finally drove home, I felt like I could see the arrows scrolling down my windshield the whole way home."

Hunter snorted. "Well, what time did you leave?"

"When it ended at five am, of course," she said with a grin.

"Well, no wonder. Even at eighteen, staying awake for over twenty hours will have you seeing things."

She sighed. "We were so resilient back then. I'm lucky if I make it to two am these days."

"Two am? That's easy."

Shocked, Gianna frowned. "You don't seriously stay up that late, do you? Don't you operate heavy machinery?"

"Rarely, if ever," he said with a laugh. "We only do home renovations. Large equipment use is rare."

"Boo! Boring!"

He laughed again. "So, you became addicted to DDR after one night at Golf Land. Did you go out and buy a system the next day?"

She snorted. "I wish. It took me over a year to save before I bought it."

"Damn. Your parents wouldn't buy it for your birthday or Christmas?"

"Princess Fiona Sally Cameron Renee Maffucci, leave that damn plant alone!"

Hunter blinked. "Uhm…who?"

"The damn cat. Give me a second."

There was a moment of silence before he heard the barest sound of paws pattering across the floor.

"Sorry. Fiona likes to abuse the one plant I've managed to keep alive."

"You have a cat?"

"Two. Fiona and Shrek."

"Ah, like the movie."

"Exactly! So, you don't operate heavy machinery. Any scandalous home renovation stories?"

"My friend Todd was involved in plenty at his old job."

"Ooh," she cooed. "Do tell?"

"They're not that exciting. Todd is just a prick who likes sleeping with women he shouldn't."

She couldn't help lift an eyebrow even though she knew he couldn't see it. "And you call that man a friend? Birds of a feather, Hunter. Birds of a feather!"

He snorted. "Not in this case. I'm nothing like him."

"Uh huh."

"So, you work at Intel?" He asked, wanting to change the subject.

"Yep. Surprised?"

"Yeah. You were terrible at math!"

Gianna cackled. "It's true though. Luckily, I had an amazing teacher."

"That's weird," he said, embarrassed. "Stop."

"You're going to have to tell me some scandalous

stories then!"

"Got none. I love the simplicity of my job. It's usually drama free. But, something related to it that is interesting is the non-profit I started. Hall's Helpers. We do small home renovations for low-income families or veterans at little to no cost. Through donations or using leftover materials from job sites, we're able to do some really great work."

"That's amazing. I love that."

"It gets better. Many of the people we hire on the non-profit arm of Hall Construction are minorities, but specifically young Black men. They're paid on-the-job apprenticeship helps them develop the skills they need to get hired anywhere or become independent contractors."

"Well, now you're just showing off," she said, more than a little impressed. "Hunter, you're really out there changing people's lives in more ways than one."

He shrugged. "I just do what I'm good at."

"Don't down play it. You change lives. You changed mine. I never got to thank you before you disappeared your senior year. That's why I went out of my way to connect with you at Valerie's party. I wanted to thank you. So. Thank you. I'm where I'm at today specifically because you had the patience and skill to teach me."

"Okay, I get it," he said, shifting uncomfortably in his seat.

She chuckled, sensing his embarrassment, and couldn't help but tease him.

"Seriously, I'm so incredibly grateful for—Hey! Did you just steal my loot?"

"Huh, you wanted that? You were so busy kissing my ass that I thought you weren't interested."

She aimed her gun at his player and opened fire. Unfortunately, his player didn't take any damage.

"Wah! Why is friendly-fire disabled!"

He laughed and kept playing. She was easy to talk to. She had always had a way of drawing him into a conversation with her friendly smile and addictive laughter. This time around, instead of staring in awe, he was an active participant in the conversation. Over the next six hours, they talked about their jobs and movies they loved and hated. They argued passionately about the best fried chicken in Sacramento and whined about the constant construction on the freeways. They kept chatting even when they paused the game to get a midnight snack, never considering calling it quits for the night.

Even when the clocked ticked to two a.m., he found himself reluctant to put an end to the easy friendship they slipped into.

"Oh my gosh!" Gianna gasped. "Hunter! It's two fricking thirty!"

"See? I told you it's easy to stay up until two."

She let out a pained groan. "I'm going to be a wreck in jiu-jitsu tomorrow."

"Jiu-jitsu? I thought you took karate?"

"I do that too, though the karate is more recent. I've been doing jitsu for…hmm…ten, no eleven years now? Yeah. I haven't been as consistent these last six years because I've been focused on karate and really, I'm just too lazy to move past purple belt."

"A purple belt in jiu-jitsu and a black belt in karate," he said, a bit shocked. "I don't know anything about their ranking systems, but both sounds incredibly impressive."

She shrugged, even though he couldn't see it. "It's

not that big of a deal. I only threw it around to scare my friend's boyfriends. My instructors wouldn't approve."

"You don't sound worried," he said when she started chuckling. "Should I be worried about getting on your bad side?"

"Sweetheart, you were already on it. Or did you forget that I knocked you on your ass with my own?"

"You know what, I think it's time for bed," he insisted, recalling that moment with a startling clarity that now suddenly had him thinking about her ass.

Gianna grinned. "Okay, but let's play again tomorrow. If you're free. I really like this game."

"Okay. Talk to you tomorrow."

"Sweet. Goodnight, Hunter!"

∞∞∞∞∞∞∞

A month flew by the same way their first night of gaming together did. Some nights they managed a few missions in two hours, while others they played until nearly three a.m. before they reluctantly went to bed. They exchanged numbers to text each other video game memes every now and then or to pick up where their late-night conversations had left off.

Hunter sometimes found it a little embarrassing that she slid so easily into his life. He gave so much of his time to work and his family, and both left him feeling happy and fulfilled. But he still had so many pockets and gaps where his life felt a little empty. Some of those gaps had been pointed out after his accident and he hadn't yet filled them completely. Gianna's bright demeanor and offering of friendship and companionship not attached to family was something he hadn't realized how much he needed. He was finally able to share a part of his life that no one else go to see.

Seeing her today for the first time since they started being true friends made him feel uncomfortably nervous, and he wasn't exactly sure why.

He was grateful that they were meeting as a group. London, and mostly Tony, invited them to watch a Kings game. Since the man was still trying to make up with London and her three besties, he rented a Loft Suite for them. Knowing he would never be willing to throw around that kind of money, Hunter didn't pass on the invitation. Fortunately for Tony, the group had decided not to have the room catered, which would have been an added cost, and chose a spot to meet up before the game.

Since everyone was getting off work from all over Sacramento, they landed on a fast casual spot near the Golden 1 Center. Frankie's Pizza was located on the corner of K Street and 2nd Street. Though it was connected to The Kay, this end, however, was home to Old Sacramento. The waterfront historic district of Old Sac was located off of Sacramento River and consisted of Gold Rush-era buildings, cobblestone streets, and all manner of restaurants, bars, and locally-owned stores. Here locals or tourists could ride on an old steam or diesel locomotive, a horse drawn carriage, or take a boat cruise.

Like all of the buildings in Old Sac, Frankie's Pizza looked like something from an old western movie. The locally owned restaurant was all modern inside, however. Hunter looked around for anyone he knew, but it looked like he was the first to arrive. He settled on ordering a beer to wait with and found a table where he could see the entrance.

As soon as he sat, London walked in with her friend Iris. Noticing him, London said something to Iris before walking over.

"Hey, Hunter," she said, embracing him in quick hug after he stood before she eased into the seat next to him. "I'd ask how it's going, but Gianna had so much to say about you last night that I don't feel like I should bother. What did you order?"

Surprised, Hunter barely stopped himself from choking on his beer. "Nothing. Better to wait and split a whole pizza since there's a bunch of us. Why were you guys talking about me? And didn't she have her big family meeting yesterday?"

"She did. She told you about her family meetings? You guys are becoming faster friends than I thought. Better late than never. She just called to tell us that since they did decide to adopt, she was considering moving too and would talk to you about renovations. Val didn't know you two were friends again, so Gianna gave us a rundown of the last month."

Hunter blinked. "Is our friendship that big of a deal?"

"To me? Yeah," she confessed, staring at him intently. "It always bothered me that you hated her. You would never tell me why and I was starting to wonder if—"

"Here, London," Iris interrupted to hand her the glass of beer. "Hunter, long time no see. Valerie's here. She said her husband isn't off yet. It feels so weird to say that. Husband. I'm going to be saying it soon. So. Weird. Anyway, how have you been?"

"I'm well. You're engaged now?" Hunter asked.

"Yep," she said, proudly holding up and wiggling her finger to show off her ring.

"How is the wedding planning going?" London asked.

Wanting no part of that conversation, Hunter quickly zoned out. When Valerie arrived with more drinks in hand, she barely spared him a greeting before diving in to talk shop.

It suddenly occurred to him that he and Gianna were the only single ones in the group. The idea of a set up made him shift uncomfortably in his seat. He glanced over at London with suspicion. She was a little too excited that he and Gianna were on friendly terms. What had she been about to say? And why was he sure he wouldn't like it?

When he glanced back toward the door, he saw a woman standing in front of the register. Though her back was to him, Hunter recognized her instantly. The cascade of soft brown curls that bounced gently with every animated gesture, the smooth lines of her long legs, and the unmistakable curve of her taut, plump ass. Even though it was October, it was still hot outside. To combat the heat, she wore simple blue jean shorts and a fitted white tank top. The casual look that somehow made her stand out even more for some reason.

The faint trace of her voice reached him. Even just the low hum of her laugh made something shift in his chest, a sudden, involuntary quickening of his heartrate. Having heard that voice in his ears so often over the last month, there was something inexplicably enticing about hearing it while basking in her effortless beauty.

She leaned slightly over the counter, speaking

animatedly with the young man behind it. It was a clean-cut kid who looked barely out of college. Was she flirting with him? His brows drew together and his jaw tightened. The guy couldn't have been more than twenty-two, tops. Still, there was an ease to the way she smiled at him that grated on his nerves.

Irritation prickled beneath his skin, irrational and fast-moving, and he scowled before he could stop himself. Why the hell did it bother him so much? There was a part of him that wanted to storm across the room and insert himself between them. But instead, he stayed rooted where he was, fuming silently, and wondering where exactly this misplaced jealously was coming from.

"Why are you making that face?" London asked.

"Huh?" He turned and quickly wiped the frown from his face. "Just wondering when Gianna will be done flirting with that kid so I can order another beer."

She blinked in surprise and looked at Gianna before looking back at him. "What makes you think she's flirting with him?"

He didn't actually know how to respond to that, so he didn't.

London read plenty into his silence however. "Interesting. Could it be that this whole time you've just been j—"

"Hello, hello!" Gianna called cheerily and went to embrace Iris. "Andy said you hadn't ordered yet, so I ordered a bunch of everything."

Valerie rose to wait for her to release Iris. "Andy? How are you already on a first name basis with the cashier?"

London glanced at Hunter before rising to get a hug too, clearly indicating he wasn't off the hook.

"I am also curious. How many degrees of separation is this?"

Gianna grinned as she squeezed London. "You've been stuck on that since Tony."

"You'll never convince me that we aren't all connected in some way with ten degrees of separation or less." She pushed Gianna toward Hunter. "Here, I'll move down so you can say hi to Hunter."

"Ah, my new online bestie, in the flesh. You don't have to get up," she said. When he stood anyway, she gave him a big hug, lingering for a moment because it just felt right. "Nice to see you."

"You too."

The scent of her made him want to grind his teeth together. His hands twitched slightly. He suddenly realized he wanted to draw her closer and hold her a little longer. He cleared his throat and tried to find his calm when she finally released him.

"I'm going to get another beer. Anyone else want more?"

They all passed since they had done more wedding talk than drink so he left to get a refill for himself.

"Well? How many degrees?" Valerie asked, curious now.

"Hmm?" She asked before pulling her gaze away from Hunter. "Oh. I tutored his girlfriend when she was in high school. When his sister needed help, she told him about me and Andy reached out. So, I guess that makes one degree of separation? Or two?" She shrugged and then sang, "It's a small world after all."

"Connected by his girlfriend," London said, wishing Hunter had heard.

"He seems pretty young," Iris noted. "Why didn't their parents reach out to you?"

"There's a lot of drama between them and unfortunately, his sister is having a hard time with it all. She's coming around though, mostly thanks to her brother."

"And you, I'm sure." Valerie reached over to take her hand. "I'm glad they have you."

Gianna squeezed her hand and smiled, knowing she hinted at something deeper.

"I do what I can. No big deal," she insisted. "So, what did I miss? What were you all talking about?"

"My wedding," Iris beamed.

"Happy for you, but pass," she said, smiling up at Hunter as he returned and sat next to her. "Hunter and I will gladly bow out of that conversation to talk about video games."

London laughed. "You nerds."

Hunter snorted. "Says the woman whose apartment has more Star Wars memorabilia than square footage."

"Right?" Gianna leaned in to him as she cackled in amusement. "What nerve. It's so comforting having someone who is finally on my side!"

"You two can talk about games another time. Gianna, you're such a social butterfly," London said, and leaned forward to look around Gianna and at Hunter. "Why don't you and Hunter spend a little time at the bar. Maybe you can find this poor guy a date."

"I think Tony would be a better wing man," Hunter said, wondering what London was up to.

"Hey," Gianna frowned, incredibly bothered by the idea of someone potentially taking what little time she had with Hunter. She looped her arm through his to cling to him. "It's not easy finding someone to game with! Stay single for me a little bit longer, okay, Hunter?"

"You're both ridiculous." Hunter bumped her with his shoulder, pulling his arm away.

Gianna laughed and let him go. "Oh, hey, I have something work related to ask you. It's kind of wild, at least to me, so I don't want you to give me an answer today."

"Go on." He sipped his drink while he waited, needing to douse the fire that her touch ignited.

"My sister and her family decided to adopt and that means they want to move into a bigger house, which will likely be a fixer upper. Remember I told you that I wanted to find a bigger space for myself too so I could have a brick and mortar space for Count Her In?"

"Yeah, I remember. You plan to move into your sister's place once she moves and want my help with the renovations?"

"That probably would have been a good idea too, but I've got something crazier in mind. Mostly due to your fence project in Valerie and Ruben's backyard. We want to buy a triplex, or maybe even a fourplex. Half for my sister and half for me and Count Her In."

"You two are closer than you let on," he said, smiling gently. "That's a great idea. Hardly crazy at all."

"Because that's not the crazy part. I want you to come house hunting with us."

"Huh? What for?"

"Renovating a house is already a big project, and for someone like me, I've got grandiose dreams that likely aren't entirely possible or fiscally responsible. It would be easier for all of us if you were there to give us a realistic idea of what can and can't be done with the building if we were to buy it. Obviously, we would pay Hall Construction for that bit of prework. I don't know how all of that works, or if what I'm asking is even in the scope of something you've done or would do, but it would mean a lot to me if we could make it happen. There's no one else I could trust with this."

A myriad of emotions blew through him at once, none of them tied to the very logical project she laid out for him. He could only stare at her while he struggled to find something to say. When she smiled sweetly at him, her eyes sparkling with affection, and patted his leg, her touch brought him back to reality.

The only problem was, this reality held a truth he wasn't ready to face.

"Don't answer now. The rule in our family is that we always take a month to really consider big decisions, so I'll bring it up later. Okay?"

He was saved from answering when Andy came to deliver pizza, wings, and a handful of appetizers. Sometime during their conversation, Jun had shown up. The restaurant buzzed with laughter, clinking glasses, and the smell of grease and garlic. As the night wore on, plates of half-eaten pizza and baskets of saucy wings crowded the table, and empty glasses of beer left wet rings on the wood.

Throughout dinner, Gianna found herself increasingly aware of Hunter. He was close. Close enough that she could feel the heat radiating off him. Close enough that every time he shifted or leaned forward, the scent of his skin and whatever clean soap he used made her stomach flutter. She knew she was approaching dangerous territory at Valerie's party. But now, being near him again, the attraction was…different.

In high school, her crush on him had felt more like an obligation. Older, smart, and hot tutor? Pure teenage girl fantasy right there. In Hawaii, the instant attraction had come naturally and had showed itself again at Valerie's party.

Over the last month, she had come to know Hunter on a personal level. She admired and respected his passion for helping vulnerable communities while simultaneously supporting the futures of young Black men. Then throw in all the other things they had in common. Opposites may attract, but they were so similar in so many ways that the more time they spent together, the more their friendship came as natural as breathing air.

All of these facts in combination with his physical presence made it difficult for Gianna to follow the conversation across the table. Valerie was telling a story about a school mishap, and everyone burst into laughter, but her smile was automatic, delayed. Her heart was too busy thudding in her chest to keep up.

Hunter's arm brushed against hers as he reached for another slice, and she felt it like a live wire along her skin. She shifted in her seat, crossing and uncrossing her legs under the table. His hand was drumming lightly against his pint glass and she envied that glass in a way that wasn't healthy.

What is wrong with me? she thought, pressing her knees together under the table. But she knew exactly what was wrong. She wanted him and it was foolish to continue to deny it. It was physical, urgent, an ache in her chest and lower still, an itch under her skin. She wanted to touch him. She wanted him to touch her.

Gianna took a long sip of her beer, hoping it would cool her down. It didn't. She glanced at him from the corner of her eye. Was it her imagination or did he look as high strung as she felt?

She all but jumped away from the group when it was

finally time to leave. She needed to get away from him for a moment to just think. To calm down. They were friends now. She couldn't and wouldn't mess that up by debasing it with her one-sided attraction.

But even outside, where the crisp fall air embraced her like a warm hug, she still felt his pull.

"I forgot that I wanted to talk to Andy before I left," Gianna said. "It shouldn't take long so I'll catch up with you."

Jun paused, throwing his arm around Valerie's waist as she turned back. "We'll wait."

"No, it's fine. Go on," she insisted and went back inside, closing the door as if that would be the end of it.

"Hunter, you stay with her," London demanded.

Tipsy, he frowned. He didn't like that idea at all, but his traitorous friend was already leading the group away while they all agreed that she had come up with the perfect solution.

The alcohol buzzed pleasantly in his head, and his attraction to Gianna was harder to ignore. An attraction that had probably been there since she first stared up at him in that bridesmaid gown on the beach in Hawaii.

Scowling, he turned to stare at the door, deeply annoyed that she had once again charmed him. It was worse this time. This time he knew more about her. Knew they had likes, interests, and hobbies in common. Knew how selflessly she helped other women step into their own brilliance with confidence. How easily she enticed him. How pathetically he fell for it all again.

He knew, even as he opened the door, that he was about to do something stupid. Something he would regret. But he was too incensed to stop himself from executing this bad decision. She had no right making him want her.

She was waiting in front of the cash register, her back to the door, but she turned when she heard it open. Her face lit with surprise before it quickly transformed into a wobbly smile. He was too caught up in his own feelings to notice the nervous way she looked at him.

"Hunter," she chastised. "You didn't have to wait."

"Yeah, well, they made me wait," he scowled. "Are you done throwing yourself at that kid?"

Her smile faded and the color drained from her face.

"Come again?"

Hunter rolled his eyes in annoyance. "Flirting with every guy you come across. You haven't changed since high school. At all."

Gianna stared at him, too stunned to speak. It wasn't just his words that shocked her. Unexpectedly, this unintended confession was like a knife to her heart and naturally the pain left her in shock. The man she was desperately attracted to, the man she respected and admired, who had changed the course of her life so dramatically that she wouldn't be who she was today if not for him…this man believed all of those filthy high school rumors about her. Moreover, he still thought they were true today.

She wasn't sure how long they stood there staring at each other, but it was Andy that brought her back to her senses.

"Hey, Gianna. Sorry, that took so long. Thanks for waiting."

She cast one last look at Hunter before forcing a

smile on her face.

"Not a problem. So, how did it go?"

"B+. She got a B+," he said, his voice filled with pride and awe. "You really pulled this off."

Gianna grinned and shook her head. "Seriously, it was a joint effort, and Abby still did most of the heavy lifting."

Andy shook his head. "You don't give yourself enough credit. The rest of her grades have come up as well. She's getting to be her old self again."

"Joint effort," she insisted. "Having such an incredible big brother through all of this is also why. Divorce can be hard for children, no matter how old they are."

He nodded solemnly. "Yeah, you're right. Anyway, you sure I can't pay you?"

"Andy, stop bringing that up. That's not how I run my business."

He tried laughing, feeling awkward. "Right, right. I knew you'd say that so I asked the chef to bake these for you. A few chocolate chip cookies for the road."

"Well, I won't say no to that," she said, taking the bag and putting it on her wrist. "I'll see you around."

"Bye, Gianna. Thanks again."

Gianna turned and walked toward Hunter, who was still standing in front of the door looking like the complete dumb fuck that he was. His sickly expression let her know he knew that he had messed up majorly. Wanting to twist the knife the same way it felt twisted in her own heart, she paused and turned back.

"Oh, Andy. Tell your girlfriend I said hi."

Andy beamed. "Will do!"

CHAPTER 7

She was across the street by the time Hunter snapped out of it and gave chase.

"Gianna!"

Ignoring him, she made her way toward the K Street Tunnel. This pedestrian only tunnel was located under the I-5 freeway and connected Old Sac to DOCO, which in turn led out to The Kay. It was well lit with colored LEDs and the walls were decorated with beautiful, lively murals.

Any other day, she might have appreciated the art, but she had finally moved past the hurt. Gone were those buzzing, unsettling feelings of lust that were strangling her with its intensity inside the restaurant. Now, she settled forcibly into anger. It was much more comfortable. She was concocting her payback when he grabbed her arm.

Her first thought was to deck him, but inspiration struck. He thought she was a flirt? Some sort of seductress who threw herself at men, letting them do to her whatever they pleased? Fine. That was exactly who she would be then.

She turned suddenly, and they collided as a result.

The hand that had grabbed her arm inadvertently slid around her waist and grasped for purchase on the small of her back. Her hands landed on his stomach, slid up to rest over on his chest. She stared up at him and let a pout settle on her lips.

"You're so mean, Hunter. You think I'd flirt with someone else's man when I've got this attractive package right here?"

Hunter froze in surprise for a brief moment before practically jumping back away from her.

Gianna grinned and slipped her arm through his, pressing the side of her breast against him. She clicked her tongue as she led him down the tunnel.

"Don't be like that. I'm happy you have a crush on me."

Surprised again, he stopped trying to wiggle out of her hold. "I don't."

Keeping his arm hooked through hers, she reached into the bag for a cookie.

"Liar. Don't be like that," she repeated. "Want a cookie?"

"No," he said, trying to pull his arm free again. She merely flexed her bicep and effectively tightened her grip. "Gianna—"

He was cut off by her small moan of pleasure and the feel of her breasts as she squirmed against his arm. His entire body flushed with heat as he tensed and hardened in response.

"It's so good," she said and gave another hum of pleasure. "Want some?"

While he was frozen in shock, she brought the bitten cookie up toward his mouth, her eyes soft and focused on his lips. She licked her own lips, the movement slow and tantalizing as the cookie touched his mouth.

"Stop," he whispered, his voice desperate and pained.

"You don't want it?"

Not like this! His voice shouted in his head. But his eyes dipped down to her lips and he leaned in, slowly closing the distance between them.

"I'll finish myself then," she breathed. Then she popped the rest of the cookie in her mouth before pulling him along again.

They didn't speak again as they walked arm in arm through the tunnel. His thoughts were reeling as he began to sober. The alcohol had loosened his tongue and created just enough space for him to shove his whole fucking foot into his mouth. Naturally, she was making him pay for his mistake.

This Gianna was nothing like the girl he knew from high school. Whatever the rumors had said, she had never been this person with him. The sweet girl he had tutored in high school had always been friendly. Her eyes kind and her demeanor gentle. Sometimes she talked more than she listened, but he always remembered her being infinitely kinder than most girls her age.

It was one of the reasons why the rumors had caught him so completely off guard. That and believing she had purposefully enchanted him into falling for her. But it had to have been a lie. Just like this behavior was a lie.

It was only a brief ten-minute walk from Old Sac to the Golden 1 Center, but it felt they had walked a hundred miles. She released him as they approached the security line.

"Gianna," he said quietly. "I'm sorry."

She felt the prick of tears as she lifted the strap on her purse to be inspected. Instead of waiting for him, she retrieved her phone to present her ticket. Desperate to get away from him, from the pain she was inflicting on both of them, she headed toward the bar.

Again, he grabbed her arm. "Where are you going? The suites are this way."

Gianna yanked her hand away and tossed her hair over her shoulder to smile at him. "Hmm? It's either the bar or a nice, dark corner. With you."

"Gianna, seriously," he said, his voice tinged with regret. "You can stop now."

"Stop what?" Walking away, she added, "It's like you said. I haven't changed."

∞∞∞∞∞∞

London and Iris were the only ones in the group with previous experience in the Golden 1 Arena suites. Though this Loft Suite was smaller, it was no less impressive. Large taupe tiles climbed the walls, and a long strip of white light lit the space in welcome. A narrow floating cabinet with a taupe quartz countertop covered the entirety of the back all. Had they bothered with catering, this is where their food would have been served. There was as a single TV screen on the wall that separated their loft from the other.

Any other day, he would have been excited by this new experience, but the more he looked, the more anxious he felt. With just eight seats, there was a spot for each of them. Hunter figured it made more sense for two of the couples to take the four deep brown leather arm chairs in the first row, while he sat in one of the four barstools right behind them.

Unfortunately, that meant it was likely that he would end up sitting next to Gianna.

He was still reeling from their earlier interaction. The feel of her breasts against him. Her floral scent, sweet and soft, wafting over to invade his nostrils. Those plump, cookie crumbed lips begging to be kissed. He had already been forced to the precipice of reality the moment he saw her again, but the way she actually flirted with him, even as retribution, pushed him right over the edge to face the truth.

Sober now, he could no longer run from it. All the stereotyping and sexist attitude he directed at her revealed itself as a convenient excuse to punish her because he was drawn to her. Then and now.

The truth was, she had never done anything specific to arouse these feelings. He simply wanted her all to himself, then and now.

Except the now was different. Now, he knew even more about her. They had so much in common and were building a very solid and entertaining friendship around it. She was even putting her trust in him to help her build a home and a space for her business. He didn't want to complicate it, but even before he stuck his foot in his mouth, his feelings would have eventually.

As expected, the couples paired up, leaving just one empty seat between him and London. He chose the end seat and, grateful that the barstools weren't built into the ground, moved his stool so that it was angled on the corner.

"Why did you move your chair like that?" London asked, eyeing him with increased suspicion.

Hunter tried to remain nonchalant. "More leg room."

She was going to say something more, but Gianna finally returned.

"Oh, man. This is sweet," she said, as she took in their surroundings. "Maybe we don't mind Tony being a fuck up after all."

Tony cringed. "My bank account won't survive any more fuck ups."

"I guess you're right," she said with a grin and dropped into the chair between London and Hunter. "Our sweet London is so expensive. Can't you think of other ways to extract payment? I know I can."

London laughed at her suggestive smile. "Your mind is filthy. Where did you go anyway?"

Gianna looked over at Hunter, her smile no less suggestive. "To the bar. I tried to get Hunter to come along so I could find him a date, like you suggested, but he refused. So, I went and got a few dates myself."

"Yeah, right," London said, rolling her eyes.

"Hunter, why are you sitting so far away? I promise I won't try to set you up with anyone. Come closer," she crooned and scooted her chair closer before pulling on his.

"Yeah, don't be so weird about it, Hunter," London grinned.

Hunter continued to be weird around Gianna and London was happy to help him pay for it by forcing him to interact with her friend. She also thought that Gianna was acting weird now. There was a feral, almost unkind look in her eyes and it was aimed at Hunter. She would just let her torture him a little bit more before she intervened.

And torture him she did. Throughout the first half

of the game, Gianna found every excuse to grab his arm or brush a hand against his thigh. Somehow, their chairs ended up even closer, forcing their thighs to touch and allowing her the opportunity to press her breasts against his arm whenever she leaned over. Whenever he made the mistake of looking at her, she looked directly into his eyes or let hers linger purposefully on his lips.

Logically, he knew she was fucking with him, but that didn't stop him from growing hard.

When they were sitting next to each other at the restaurant, she barely touched him. On the occasion their eyes had met, there was never anything suggestive or wanton behind her eyes. He could see, clear as day, the difference in her interactions with him, and hell, even Andy and the way she was currently behaving. At the restaurant, she had been friendly, respectful, kind. Now? She was a vindictive seductress.

He had to check the urge to respond in kind. To grab a fistful of her those gorgeous flowing curls, yank her against him, and punish her with a brutal kiss. The image was so clear, coupled with the sound of her moaning. He wondered how he managed to keep his hands to himself.

I'm so fucked, he thought.

"Well, it's halftime on the court, but it's game time for me," Gianna declared as she rose from her seat as if she hadn't been practically rubbing against Hunter for an hour. "I'm heading back up to the bar."

Valerie blinked in surprise as she watched her go. Concerned, she went over to London.

"What's with Gianna?" Valerie asked her. "She's being weird."

"Yeah, I agree. Let's go find out, Hunter."

He was literally pulled from his thoughts when London grasped his arm. She tugged until he rose from the seat and led him out the door. In the hallway, the noise from the arena bowl was slightly muted.

"What happened? And don't play dumb. I know both of you too well so I know something definitely happened between you two."

Hunter shifted on his feet, trying to decide how much to tell her and hide his boner as well. Thankfully, London merely stared at him, crossing her arms over her chest as she waited.

"I said something I shouldn't have," he said eventually.

"Did you tell her why you've hated her for so long?"

He sighed. "I don't hate her. Not anymore."

"Oh, really?" London asked, raising an eyebrow. "So, it is what I thought. What your face confirmed when she was talking to Andy. You did have a crush on her, and hated her for it."

"It was high school," he sighed in frustration. "Who didn't?"

Her eyes instantly turned cold in fury. "Very few people had a genuine crush on Gianna. The rest? They just wanted to see if the rumors were true. Too many people treated her like they were truth instead, even without evidence. It pisses me off to think that you were one of them."

He looked down in shame. "Look, I'm so—"

"I'm not the one who needs an apology. You better fix it, Hunter."

Though she didn't say it, he heard the threat. Too bad he didn't know how he would fix things. Or even if he could.

∞∞∞∞∞∞

Before the start of the game, she became that woman Hunter expected her to be, flirting and teasing men without shame or interest. At the time, she half expected him to follow her, or maybe she hoped he would. Nevertheless, she only lasted playing that game for about fifteen minutes before she finally made her way to the suite.

Now, back at the bar, she had no expectation of being followed. Though she was still uninterested in any man's attention, she didn't really want to be near him without the distraction of the game. Too many prying eyes. She was certain London had picked up on it and she would have to explain later.

Annoyed with herself, Gianna stared aimlessly down at the arena bowl from the Sierra Nevada Draught House, an impressive bar with an even more impressive view, and sipped on a glass of wine. She could see that some people remained in their seats, enjoying the halftime show, while others ventured out for food and drink. The noise was near deafening from this vantage point, and it was exactly what she needed right now.

She hadn't felt this way in a long time. Maybe even since high school, and she didn't like it one bit. Normally, she would go to her friends to distract her, but life wasn't so simple anymore. Between their careers and relationships, she couldn't monopolize their time venting about other people's cruelty. And since Hunter was a cousin and a good friend, she didn't want to taint their relationships with her negative experience.

She never imagined that Hunter would fall into that group. In high school, Hunter was the quiet and shy kid, and he had always struck her as kind and steadfast. He hadn't run with any rowdy crowds and would probably have been described as a straight up nerd. Up until his senior year, whenever she was with Valerie and London, at least half the times he was also there. How had he come to not only hear those rumors, but also believe them after spending so much time with her?

Other than Ruben, Hunter was the only guy she felt saw her for who she really was and not who vindictive gossips and sadistic boys said she was. It was incredibly disheartening to realize how wrong she had been about him.

Yeah, it had definitely been years since she felt this coalescence of anger and hurt.

"Hey! Hey you! Eliana!"

Gianna's face scrunched, annoyed by the loud voice. A bar this big, and somehow this guy was so close he was practically yelling at her. She stood straight, planning to move further down, when the owner of that voice stepped beside her.

"I'm talking to you. What you can't hear now?" He asked with a sneer.

She looked him over and then remembered he had hit on her when she came to the bar earlier.

"I heard you, but I'm not Eliana."

This only made him angrier and he leaned forward aggressively, crowding her space. "Oh, so you give out fake names and numbers? Stupid bitch."

"I told you my name is Gianna. Gianna," she said it slowly, emphasizing the syllables. She leaned back over the railing, dismissing him. "Eliana is close, but also, not really."

"Like I'm going to fall for that after you gave me a fake number," he sneered. "You think you're something, huh? You're nothing but a whore."

She couldn't remember whether or not she had given him a fake number, but given his attitude she assumed she had. He reeked of alcohol and too much cologne. He was decently attractive, but there was something about him that screamed red flag. His behavior now proved she made the right decision.

Worried that she wasn't in the right mindset to handle this exchange without resorting to violence, Gianna put her glass down and stood. The moment she stepped back, she backed into someone, though there hadn't been anyone there a moment ago. She felt a quick trickle of fear.

"Gianna."

The familiar masculine voice was deep and dangerously close to her ear. It sounded both angry and regretful, impatient and chastising. Fear transformed to curiosity. Before she could turn to see his face, a hand fisted in her hair, trapping her in place. She immediately lifted one hand to grasp that hand and elbowed his stomach. She was about to twist away when she heard her name again, this time recognizing that voice.

"Gianna," Hunter grunted, tightening his grip and stepping even closer.

Their bodies pressed together intimately and his breath fanned over her ear. Shocked, she stopped struggling, and felt her heart try to beat out of her chest when his other hand caught her hip and held her in place.

Hunter tipped his head down, his lips ghosting over

her ear as he whispered, "Stop struggling."

For some reason, that made her resist more. She tried moving away again, but he only pulled her head back further, exposing her neck. He dipped his head and his lips caressed her suddenly sensitive skin. Startled, aroused, she arched her back, trying to escape those lips, and inadvertently pressed her butt against his crotch. His arm came around her waist to hold her in that precarious position.

"Play along," Hunter demanded harshly, sliding his thumb under the hem of her tank top until he felt skin.

Her eyes widened further in surprise, and she wasn't sure if it was because of this game he was playing or because she found herself suddenly aroused by it.

"Hunter…" she managed, finally finding her voice. "What are you—"

"What are *you* doing? Did I give you permission to talk to this man again?"

She couldn't help but tremble. That husky, commanding voice. Those soft lips wreaking havoc as they whispered over her skin. His hand, now fully under her shirt, splayed across her belly. And the bulge she felt pressed against her ass was evidence of his own arousal. Trembling was the least she could do when it took all of her strength not to moan and beg him for more.

What the fuck was wrong with her?

"Who the fuck are you?" Demanded the other man, finally remembering that he had a voice.

Hunter glared at him, but otherwise ignored him. Caught up in this game, in the feel of Gianna trapped against him, just the way he wanted, he took more liberties than he deserved and pressed a kiss to her neck.

"Did you give him the wrong number like I told you to?"

She had so many questions. How long had he been listening to their conversation? Where did he find the fucking nerve to manhandle her this way? What the hell did it say about her that she found this so goddamn sexy? Why was she wishing he would yank her head back and capture her lips instead?

"Answer me," he demanded, his grip tightening in her hair again.

"Y-yes," she stammered, barely managing to suppress a moan.

"Good girl," he chuckled, enjoying this entirely too much. "I'll have to reward you later."

"What kind of kinky shit are you two into?" The stranger asked.

Gianna had the same question.

Hunter stared at the other man as he released Gianna's hair. He placed his hand on her chin and, slowly and deliberately, turned her head toward him. Knowing this might be the last time he'd get to touch her, he leaned in and pressed his lips to the corner of her mouth. It was soft at first and it was truly all he intended to do.

But something inside him broke open and the kiss deepened before he could stop it. His hand slid to her throat, his touch more possessive now, his hunger impossible to disguise.

He knew it was wrong. Knew he didn't have the right. Not anymore, maybe not ever. But the taste of her was addictive and in that moment, with another man still watching and time slipping away like sand through his fingers, he didn't care about right or wrong. He just needed her to feel it, to know she was his, even if only for this stolen second.

Not a single thought passed through her head as he devoured her. Possessed her, and set fire to every nerve in her body. Instead, she surrendered willingly, as if she had no free will at all. As if this man had captured her mind, body, and spirit. When he finally broke the kiss, her mind continued to remain blank.

Returning to his senses, Hunter looked up to see that the man was still there. The look he sent him was withering, and the poor guy actually stepped back in response.

"What are you still doing here?" Hunter growled. "Get the fuck out of here. And think twice before getting so aggressive with another man's woman."

"B-b-but she was flirting with me," he stammered.

"I don't give a fuck about what you *thought* she was doing. She gave you the wrong number, probably because you begged like the pathetic piece of shit you are. The next time it happens, and I know it will happen again, give up and move on. Don't call her a bitch or a whore, don't get in her face. Take the L and move the fuck on."

He finally released Gianna to take her hand. Stunned, aroused, and utterly devastated, she followed dumbly as he led her away. It wasn't until he released her hand after they stopped at the elevator that she seemed to be able to form thoughts and words again.

"What the fuck was that?" she demanded.

Hunter flicked his eyes over to her briefly before turning back to push the call button again. "Overly aggressive guys like that are like lion cubs trying to stake new territory. They get real cooperative when a dominate male comes along."

"That doesn't explain why you fucking manhandled

me that way. Why you…why you…"

Kissed wasn't the right word when she still felt like her every nerve ending was shouting his praises.

Hunter rocked on his heels. "Maybe I just wanted to."

Gianna pictured herself wringing his neck, but for some reason, her body stayed rooted in place as she gaped at him in shock.

"I was just trying to get rid of the guy," he explained.

"And saying 'go away' never occurred to you?"

"No," he confessed. He had wanted his hands on her, so he put them on her. "Not at all."

"You fucker!"

"Didn't you spend the last hour making sure I wanted to do just that?"

Hunter looked over at her when she didn't respond.

"I don't want to play this game with you, Gianna." He held his hands out in frustration. "I get it. I fucked up. You've proved your point. Can we move past this now?"

"Move past this?" She laughed, the sound dark with anger. "First you basically call me a flirtatious whore and then you treat me as one to scare off another man. You think we can move past this?"

He stared at her dumbly, realizing suddenly that he further fucked an already fucked up situation. When the elevator finally arrived, she breezed past him as if he wasn't even there. They rode in silence. Once on their floor, she went to the restroom, leaving him to return on his own.

The game had started up again by then. Seeing him return alone, London glared at him.

Knowing he had made things go from bad to worse,

he could only shake his head in response and sat down at the bar.

"She's in the bathroom."

London retrieved Valerie and the two of them left the suite. A moment later, Jun stood behind Hunter and Tony.

"Can you two dumbasses stop fucking up with your women? Every time you do, they take mine away from me," Jun complained.

Tony turned, hands up in defense. "I didn't do anything this time!" Then he looked at Hunter. "I didn't realize you and Gianna—"

"We're not," Hunter interrupted. "I don't know why he thinks that."

Jun grinned. "Lots of little puzzle pieces that are only coming together just now."

"Do tell," Tony said.

Hunter snorted, desperate to change the subject. "Or don't."

"For starters, you went to high school and college with London," Jun pointed out. "Did anything ever happen between the two of you? A little kiss, a one-night stand?"

"What?" Hunter hiss, appalled. "No, never. Why would you think that?"

"Why not? This dumbass over here fell for her after only talking to her for an hour and you tell me that after years of being around her, nothing happened between you two?"

"I feel both relief and suspicion," Tony said, considering. "I know she wasn't mine then, and I'm really glad you didn't, but he kind of has a point. Why wouldn't you? I mean, look at her."

"Oh, come on! You're in love with her, of course

you would say that."

"I figured he was gay or he was dating or interested in someone else. And after today, I can't help but think that someone else is Gianna," Jun said, rocking on his heels. "I don't know what happened between you two since we left the restaurant, but it's enough to take my wife and his girlfriend away."

"But London said that Hunter always kind of hated Gianna," Tony said thoughtfully. Then it clicked. "*Oh.*"

"Oh what?" Hunter demanded, a little panicked. "You're reading into things."

"And another piece of the puzzle is added. Seems like that hate was a cover," Jun said. "That's a long time to carry a torch. Did your arms finally get tired and you decided to put those hands to better use?"

"That's such a reach," Hunter scowled, annoyed because that was basically exactly what had happened.

"Is it though? Well, there is one last damning piece of evidence that will prove my theory beyond a reasonable doubt. Oh, and here it is now," Jun said with a wide grin as he turned toward the door.

Gianna had walked in, her gaze carefully blank as she looked ahead with her friends right behind her. London and Valerie, however, stared at them, their eyes full of violence. If looks could kill, they would have suffered a painful death. Or rather, since they were aimed at one man in particular, he would have been down on his knees, begging for mercy.

"And there it is," Jun said quietly. "I'll say it again. Stop fucking up with your woman."

Tony actually shuddered in fear. "Oh, fuck. What did you do?"

"I—I," he stammered. "It's…"

He didn't even know what to say.

"Damn," Evan, Iris' fiancé, said, joining them at the bar. "Who hurt Gianna? I haven't seen London that pissed in a long time."

Tony and Jun stared silently at Hunter, eventually drawing Evan's gaze as well.

"Oh," he said. "I didn't realize you two were seeing each other."

Hunter groaned in defeat and for what felt like the millionth time that night he faced an unfortunate truth.

I'm so fucked.

CHAPTER 8

Gianna drummed her fingers against the steering wheel as she stared at the old two-story tri plex across the street. On the outside, there was nothing about the home that appealed to her, but since *he* had insisted that it was worth seeing, here she was.

It had been three weeks since she had spoken to him. She didn't count the one and only text message he had sent her as a conversation. As expected, he didn't respond to the eggplant and peach emojis that she sent in response. She didn't know if he reached out to her on PlayStation either since she remained offline every weekend. It was easy to avoid someone who wasn't really all that integrated into her life.

While she hadn't forgotten that she had asked to hire him, she figured it was best if they just left the whole idea alone. If she avoided him for a whole month, he would assume that she was no longer interested in hiring him.

Unfortunately, that plan didn't pan out.

Thanks to London, who was always looking to connect people to resources and information, Sam was very familiar with Hall Construction. In fact, over the last five years, both 360 Realty and Hall Construction passed along each other's business cards to their respective clients. Sam had been too excited about the family agreeing to adopt when Gianna had mentioned Hunter so it wasn't until she looked at the business card Gianna had left behind that she realized the connection. A quick call to the office, and Ms. Juanita, Hunter's mother, was more than happy to acquiesce to the request.

And so, here they were, ahead of schedule, about to tour their first home.

She still wasn't ready to face Hunter. Her feelings for him were so complicated now and she was still struggling to sort them out.

There was still a lot of hurt and anger knowing that he had always believed those rumors about her. His sudden disappearance in high school, the standoffish way she dismissed her in Hawaii. His aggressive and sexist stance when they bumped in to each other. Even the way he avoided her at Valerie's party. Each moment made a sick kind of sense now. He probably resented the fact that he had ever been attracted to her and wanted to stay away from her.

That night at the Kings game proved he still wanted her, and he couldn't be happy about it.

And that was the other hurdle. Despite the hurt, the anger, and the sense of betrayal, she still wanted him. Maybe more so because she realized that she had a level of comfort with him that she hadn't felt with a man in a long time.

The usual fear she had when someone, especially a man, came up behind her had been fleeting. It was certainly true that over the years, that fear had diminished to something that was highly manageable. It was on very rare and specific occasions, like when

Hunter grabbed her at Valerie's house, that she had an intense, fearful reaction. But at the game, there had been only a brief moment of fear, and it was gone almost as soon as she registered it.

Instead, she had been aroused by his aggressive and controlling manhandling. She suspected that he didn't have a gentle bone in his body after she crashed into him Hawaii. How was she to know that his rough and domineering behavior would turn her on? Or that she would dream of heated arguments that ended with rough sex for a week straight?

Scowling, Gianna shoved her way out of her car. Autum had finally realized it was early November and decided to take over, so she pulled a pale blue sweatshirt over her black tank, then slipped her keys and phone into the pockets of her black leggings after locking the door.

Crossing the two-lane street, she saw that the door was already open. Hunter must already be inside. Since she wasn't sure if she would punch him or pounce him, she opted to wait for her sisters outside.

Inside, Hunter angled his body away from the window, hiding himself from view, but still able to watch her. With her hair tied up in a messy bun and her face free of make-up, she reminded him of that "girl next door" trope and felt a whole new wave of guilt wash over him.

That night at the game had flung him to the bottom of the abyss inside him, where he hid all of the emotions he hadn't wanted to face. After a session with his therapist, he finally realized that he had let himself hate her, and all women like her, for seemingly giving herself to everyone but him. Trapped in the vicious cycle of misogyny, sexism, and confirmation bias, he had ruined one relationship after the other.

He had started going to therapy to start break that cycle. Now, more than ever, he had to destroy it before he ruined the one thing he had always wanted.

After London shamed him and Gianna showed him who she really was, he knew that those rumors had never been true. He wondered just how deeply he had hurt Gianna when she realized that he had never seen her for who she really was. It was unfair of him to expect her to forgive him so quickly, and he knew he had to make it up to her.

Hunter watched her face light up, her smile brightening those gorgeous eyes, when two women and a young girl walked up. She embraced each one in a lingering squeeze before attaching herself to the girl. He recognized one woman instantly as her sister, the resemblance between the two of them undeniable.

He stepped out to greet them. "Hey, good morning."

"Hunter!" Sam stepped up to shake his hand. "It's so nice to finally meet you. Ms. Juanita always talks about you—well she talks about all her kids—but we've never had the occasion to meet."

"Yeah, same," he responded, though it wasn't the same at all. His mom never told him that Sam was a woman so he just assumed Sam was a man. And now he felt like an ass for assuming their gender all over again. "Thanks for thinking of us for this."

"There really wasn't another choice. Your family's work is always stellar. This is my wife, Emilia," she said, stepping to the side so they could shake hands. "And our daughter, Ciara."

"Feels a bit weird because you're a stranger, but not?" Emilia shook his hand and then laughed at herself. "Gianna never shut up about you after you tutored her."

Hunter couldn't help but grin and looked over at Gianna. "Is that right?"

"I'm sure whatever you think is true," she said, unsmiling. "Let's go in. I'm dying to see it."

Sam and Emilia shared a look that told him the behavior Gianna just displayed was not the norm. He sighed as he followed them in. Just as he expected, she was still hurting.

He wandered the house with them, hanging back to observe them, and only speaking if they asked about renovations. They stuck together as they explored, taking turns sharing their thoughts and feelings. This would be quite the group project and from what he gleaned, they intended to try to meet everyone's wants and needs. It would definitely be a challenge, and he hoped that he could rise to the occasion.

"I'm ranking this one bottom of the list," Emilia shared as they headed out.

"I think it's too soon to say, but, I agree," Sam said with a sigh. "Thanks for telling us about it though, Hunter."

"It helped give an idea of what you don't want and that's just as important."

"Yeah, that's true," Sam agreed.

They continued to chat when the other realtor returned to lock up. While the three of them talked, Emilia led Gianna and Ciara to the sidewalk. She pulled her keys from her pocket and gave them to her daughter.

"Wait in the car for me? I'll be there in a minute."

"Okay." She gave Gianna a hug. "Bye, Zia!"

"See you later." She turned to her sister, curious.

"What's up?"

"That's what I want to know," she said, looking over at Hunter then at Gianna again.

"What? Fuck, am I that transparent?" Gianna mumbled.

"Yes!" Emilia laughed. "You always talk to everyone and anyone about anything and everything, so naturally when you don't, it sticks out. What happened? You were so excited about reconnecting with him, but you were so short with him today."

Gianna looked down and shuffled on her feet. She didn't want to lie to her sister, but didn't want to tell her what Hunter said either. She settled on telling half of the truth.

"It's complicated," she said with a frustrated sigh.

"How complicated?"

"Very," Gianna insisted.

"In what way?"

Gianna slanted her a look.

"Ooooooooooh," she said, understanding.

"We both said and did things we're regretting. I'm pretty sure we've already messed up our friendship."

"Do you like him?"

Gianna groaned. "It's complicated."

Emilia pursed her lips, sensing there was more to this that she wasn't saying. She shot a quick glance at Hunter again, curious and suspicious.

"If you think it will be a problem, we can find another construction company to work with."

Gianna looked up. "We don't need to go that far just yet."

Since there would be time to learn more later on, Emilia didn't push. Gianna wasn't ready to share yet, for whatever reason, so she would just keep a close eye on both of them for the time being.

"Hunter, thanks again," Sam said as they stopped in front of Gianna and Emilia. "I sent you a text from our new group chat so if you hear about any other properties, feel free to share. Same for you two as well."

"Got it," Hunter said, then stuffed his phone back in his pocket. "Gianna. Don't leave yet. I've got something for you. I'll see you two later."

Those mixed emotions swelled again at the sound of her name on his lips. Her heart stirred with interest, desire. Her brain held up red flags, blared sirens of warning. She didn't say anything to him as they said their goodbyes to her sister. All too soon, the two of them were alone.

"Walk with me," he commanded, and led the way to his truck. She followed slowly, but still didn't speak. "You're still mad at me. Probably hurt too, and that makes it even worse. I was wrong. And stupid. I went way to far with what I said and what I did. I don't expect you to forgive me, but I hope that you will, eventually."

Gianna stopped walking to stare at him with a frown.

Unsurprised that she would need a moment, he kept moving until he reached his truck. Once it was unlocked, he retrieved the game from the passenger door pocket. Closing it, he walked back to her.

There was a full two cars length between them. Her frown only deepened as she continued to stare. Why did she suddenly feel like he was a panther stalking his prey? His deep brown eyes fixed her in place as he strode confidently to her.

He was a full head taller than her. His long legs were

clad in grey jeans and his impressive lean figure was accented by the thin black sweater he wore. The perfect hunter. Heart pounding, she looked up at him as he stepped in front of her, and knew she was his prey. Even though she knew she was in danger, those flags stilled and those sirens quieted.

Hunter tilted his head, curious about what she was thinking. He held out the video game. "Here. Let me know when you're ready to play."

Gianna looked down at the sparkly pink bow that sat just beneath the words Vault Hunter 3. Play what, exactly? Why was she so certain that he didn't mean this video game?

"Look at me."

She sent him a look of disgust and snatched the game from him. "You're so bossy."

He grinned. "And you're such a good girl. See you later, Gianna."

Before she could retort, their attention was captured by a sudden loud noise. Hunter turned sharply in the direction it came from, recognizing the distinct and disturbing sound of metal crashing into metal. His body jerked instinctively when he saw that a car had been rear-ended, and while some part of him knew it was foolish and useless to head back there, he was tossed violently back in time nonetheless.

Eighteen months ago, he was driving his SUV down Highway 99, on his way to meet a new client. Out of nowhere, the vehicle behind him slammed into his rear bumper, hurling his body into the airbag just as it exploded from the steering wheel. The force spun his car until it came to a stop, straddling the lane at an angle.

Frozen, he stared ahead, looking straight into

oncoming traffic, just in time to see another car barreling toward him. The shriek of its brakes drowned out the music still playing from his speakers, moments before the second impact hit.

Glass exploded around him, the piercing sound like a scream in his ears as shards slashed into his face and arms. The side airbag deployed just in time. Later, they'd tell him it saved his life—kept the crushed metal door from caving his ribs and spine. Still, it shoved him hard against the center console, causing pain to radiate from every point of contact.

Then, silence. Thick and sudden. It muffled the agony enough to let him breathe for a second. But the quiet didn't last. Relief was short-lived, replaced by the noise of voices and the chaos of people working to pull him free.

"Hunter!"

How did they know my name?, he thought.

"*Hunter!*"

He sucked in a breath, only then realizing he hadn't been breathing at all. Awareness crashed back in as the present snapped into focus. Gianna's face appeared before him, tight with concern, her hands cradling his cheeks.

"Breathe. Slowly," she urged, guiding him with deep, measured breaths of her own.

Hunter tried to follow her rhythm, grounding himself. He slid his hands to her hips, leaned forward, and rested his forehead against hers. His eyes fluttered shut as his pulse began to settle. It took a long moment before he could speak.

"I'm okay now," he murmured.

Gianna searched his face, hesitant, before letting her hands fall away. She started to step back, but his grip on her hips tightened.

He wasn't ready to let go.

"Maybe you should sit down," she said softly.

"I'm okay. Seriously. This," he nodded toward their closeness. "This feels good."

She narrowed her eyes. "Are you *hitting on me* after having a damn panic attack?"

"Yes and no," he admitted, lips quirking. "It's been a while since it happened. Holding you like this…helps me come back faster."

Her expression softened. Unreasonably pleased by his confession, Gianna lifted her hand to his face again, gentle fingers brushing along his cheek.

"The accident was really that bad?"

"Yeah. It was," he said with a sigh. "I'll tell you more about it another day. The physical stuff healed, mostly. I've got a pretty wicked scar on my side. But the emotional scars? They're reminders to keep living."

Finally, he stepped back and forced himself to look toward the scene at the stop sign. Two drivers, unharmed, calmly exchanged insurance information. Just a minor fender bender. Watching them, knowing they were safe, chased away the last clinging ghosts of his own crash.

Gianna followed his gaze. "Are you sure that you're okay? I can drive you home if you need."

Hunter turned back to her. She had dropped the gift he'd brought her just to get to him faster. He stooped, picked it up, and held it out to her.

"I like that you're worried about me," he said, quieter now. "But I promise I'm okay. Thank you. For helping me."

"You probably shouldn't drive or be alone." She accepted the gift again and stared at him. "The look on your face earlier…I've never seen anyone look like that. I couldn't even reach you at first."

"Then come back to my place," he said gently. "We can play."

"Hunter," she snapped.

He sent her that cocky grin, not knowing that it wreaked havoc on her impulses. For one insane minute, she considered actually going with him.

"I meant the *video game*," he said, clearly enjoying himself. "But I wouldn't mind rewarding you for thinking otherwise."

She scowled, spun on her heel, and marched away. "Bye."

Hunter laughed, calling after her, "Call me when you're ready to play! The video game or—"

She flipped him off without looking back.

∞∞∞∞∞∞

She didn't call him, but he hadn't really expected her to. But every time he saw her or received a text from their new group chat, he wished she would. He missed her. He missed sending her some random message about stupid shit his team said. He missed how annoyed she would get when he swiped the loot before she could when they played Vault Hunter 2. He missed listening to her talk about a tutoring session. He had come to cherish and look forward to any interaction with her, no matter how small.

It wasn't enough. He recalled, far too often, how it felt when her ass was pressed against him, making him grow harder each time she exhaled. He dreamed of slipping inside her, his hand in her hair and his arm around her waist. He wanted the ownership he claimed in front of that man to be reality as he fucked them both into oblivion.

Ever since the accident, he'd craved something real. A serious relationship, not just company. He wanted someone he could talk to about everything and nothing, someone whose presence made silence feel safe and the loud feel like heaven. Someone he could hold when the weight of life pressed too hard, borrowing their strength until he found his own again.

He thought he found that in Gianna. Hoped he could have that with her. He just had to get her to forgive him so that he could convince that her she wanted the same.

Hunting for a parking space, he reminded himself to be patient. It had only been a month. Their lives were connected right now so he had time to apologize again and weaken her defenses. Like the last few weekends, Sam planned back-to-back showings for this weekend as well. As long as he kept getting in her space, she couldn't ignore him, or what was building between them.

He found a spot a few houses down and across the street in front of John C. Fremont Park. Fremont Park was located in Midtown, a neighborhood district in the downtown area of Sacramento. It was a busy area with parks, restaurants, nightclubs, and bars. The park itself hosted the Chalk It Up! Festival every year. The location definitely had a significant number of pros and cons, but he could see them enjoying living in the heart of Sacramento.

Sam had shared that this home was located in a historic district so many of the homes on this street were a mix of colonial, craftsman and other classic styles. If they chose this home, this would create some constraints. In addition to that challenge, the house had sustained significant fire damage. A house like this would, and had, scared away a lot of potential buyers.

It was three stories, with a staircase leading up to the second-floor porch. While the front of the home had minimal damage, he could tell that a significant portion of it had burned down in a fire. He stood and stared, considering, and wondered if he should run away as well.

"Hey, Hunter."

He glanced over to see Eliana walking up to him. Despite the cold December chill, her long black peacoat was unbuttoned. Beneath it, she wore a moss-colored suit and crew neck blouse in cream. She worked alongside Sam as a realtor for their company, 360 Realty, but she handled commercial real estate, while Sam did residential. Clearly, she had just finished showing a property.

"Shit, it's worse than I thought." She stared gravely at the house. "What is Sam thinking?"

Hunter chuckled. "That I'm a miracle worker? Who fed her that lie?"

"Hell if I know. I like the area though," she said thoughtfully, turning to look at the park. "Might be some room to knock down the price given the state of the house and how long it's been on the market."

"That's your lane. I'll save my thoughts on the construction for when everyone arrives."

"I told them I was running late a half hour so we could talk."

Hunter blinked. "Talk?"

"Gianna hasn't been herself since we started this,

and I had my suspicions about why, especially when she was hesitant to give me the whole story. Very unlike her," she added. "So, I went to London."

"Ah," he said, not knowing what else to say.

"Even now, after all these years, she's still putting me first," she said, frustrated and annoyed. "Still trying to protect me. She'll never tell you how those rumors got started. Because I see the way you look at her and I think she feels the same way, I'm going to tell you why. That way, what I did won't be the wall that stands between you two. That way, you'll understand why what you said hurt her so badly."

Her face suddenly turned solemn and he felt himself draw closer, wanting to comfort her but not knowing how or why he should.

"Like most kids, I had my first crush in third grade. By the time I got to fifth grade, there was no doubt in my mind that I was a lesbian. However, my family is deeply Catholic, so I also knew I couldn't be. I struggled with this, worked to suppress my attraction to girls. In high school, I met other girls that were out. To test my parents, I told them about those girls. If their stance on homosexuality hadn't been clear before, they made it so then. So, knowing my parent's love and acceptance was on the line, I convinced myself the cure was boys."

"The rumors were about you?" The shock sat fully on his face. He hadn't expected this.

"They weren't rumors. Anybody that wanted me got to have me, and in any way they wanted. The only part that was a lie was whom those rumors were about. It was never Gianna. But since we were sisters and so close in age, my crimes became hers." She started pacing, unable to stand still as the memories came rushing back. "I feel both pity and disgust for my past self. I punished myself, recklessly abused my body, and put myself in dangerous situations because I was a lesbian. Then I did it all over again as further punishment for all the shitty things I did with people I couldn't stand."

She stopped suddenly to cover her eyes. "Gianna never blamed me. If anything, the worse the rumors became, the worse her classmates, both male and female, treated her as a result, the more she stood by my side. After I graduated from high school, she and my aunt convinced me to come out to my parents. As expected, they freaked. Kicked me out. Disowned me. Forbid Gianna from seeing me, and later, my aunt because she took me in. And still, this only made her dig her heels in even further."

Her watch vibrated and she rubbed her eyes before stopping the alarm. Knowing she didn't have a lot of time left before they arrived, she continued on.

"The summer before her junior year, she got a job to establish her independence so she could file for emancipation. By the end of her junior year, our parents also disowned her and the court order was approved. Thankfully, we were able to live full time with Zia Angela by then. She was the only one who stood by us. Our entire family followed our parents lead and cut the three of us out."

Eliana sighed. "As you can imagine, things were hard for all of us, but Gianna had this powerful grit. She still does. She always keeps her pain to herself, especially if it can hurt someone else. That's why she won't tell me what you said. She doesn't want me to feel guilty. Hell, even if you asked, she wouldn't tell you the truth about the rumors just to protect me. What did she say that day? When we were at that very first house?"

"I'm sure whatever you think is true," he recalled. It had bothered him that she responded that way. Now he knew why.

"Yeah, exactly. Did she tell you that she turned down a full ride scholarship to UCLA's Computer Engineering program?"

Hunter gaped at her. "Are you serious? She could have gone to UCLA?"

With me, he thought. How different might things have been if she had gone to UCLA as well?

"She turned it down to stay with me. And still, she doesn't blame me. Even though it's mine, she won't let me take the blame. Even though she's hurting, she won't let me take the blame. You may have delivered the blow, but I was the weapon you used to hurt her. You brought back a lot of pain for her, and I'm sure it surprised her that you thought those rumors were true."

A car honked it's horn, drawing their attention. They saw Ciara and Sam wave from the passenger side windows as Gianna drove by.

Hunter sighed. "I know I hurt her. How do I fix it? How do I show her that I want her for who she is, not for who I thought she was? Do I keep apologizing?"

"She feels something for you, even if she doesn't want to. And because she does, she won't cross the line. She wants to protect you from any potential negative fallout starting a relationship with you may or may not have. Even if it hurts her, that's what she'll do. Don't let her. Get in her way. Knock down the wall even as she tries to build it. You're going to have to put up a fight to be with her, but if you can stick it out, she'll love you the way she's always loved me."

Hunter nodded, willing to take any advantage he could get. "Why do you trust me with her?"

"Because if you didn't matter to her, she would have cut you lose the minute you pissed her off. The fact that she still allows you in her life is telling. Besides, if I've made a mistake, I'll make sure we both regret it for the rest of our lives."

He laughed. "That's fair. Alright, anything else I should know?"

"If you can't win her with what I've told you, throw in the towel. Switch sides. I know a couple guys who are looking for a top just like you. You don't strike me as a bottom, but what do I know."

"Definitely not a bottom," Gianna chimed in as she caught the tail end of their conversation. "You know, I figured you wouldn't do this until after the renovations."

Hunter had to fight the urge to stare as he turned to face her. Knowing so much more now, he felt like he was seeing her for the first time and he just wanted more time to drink her in.

"So late," Sam said, interrupting his thoughts. "I assumed it would happen at least halfway through the renovations. Why are you so impatient to know this time?"

Since he couldn't be sure if they were being serious or not, Hunter feigned confusion. "Switch sides? Top and bottom? What are you even talking about?"

"Gianna, fill him in later. Sam, what the hell? Why are we looking at this dilapidated disaster?"

"Everything has potential, even a building with substantial fire damage. It took a fair amount of the back down, which is why we can't actually go in. But the façade itself is pretty well intact. There are or were five units here, with one being in what is considered a basement."

"Woah, a basement? In Sacramento?" Gianna asked.

"The city terms them delta-style or high basements," Hunter explained. "Likely a close cousin to a walkout basement. The stairs take you to what is officially considered the first floor. The entrance to the basement unit is off to the side."

They all followed the direction he was pointing before following Sam to see the back of the property.

Seizing the opportunity to get in her way like Emilia had suggested, Hunter threw his arm around Gianna's shoulder and leaned down to whisper in her ear. "So, what makes you so sure I'm a top?"

Gianna tried to elbow him away, but he only pulled her closer. He slowed their pace to a crawl, creating a distance between them and her family.

"A hard headed, domineering, and bossy piece of shit like you could only be a top," she sneered, trying to get away again. "Let go."

"As long as you know that makes you bottom," he chuckled.

"Oh, dear," she said sadly, even as her heart started beating faster. "Hunter, did you think that I was flirting with you for real? While I can't fault your taste, you should know that it'll never happen."

"It already happened, or did you forget how you trembled when I kissed you?"

"Oh, yeah. I guess you did force a nonconsensual kiss out of me. I forgot about it. For your sake."

"Gianna, you're a terrible actress," he declared. He imagined she might tremble in his arms again if nipped her ear. Worried that he would do just that, he let her go. "You think I couldn't tell, but I know what you like. Don't worry. I haven't forgotten about rewarding you."

He walked away, and again left her picturing violence but unable to follow through. She was so irritated why that kept happening, and didn't fully understand why. Maybe it was self-preservation. It was never wise to taunt a predator. But she really wanted to hurt him for making her feel this needy.

Gianna cracked her neck and rolled her shoulders, willing the sexual tension away before she started moving again.

A Sacramento Regional Transit light rail station sat directly behind the house. The crossing signal bell was ringing as the light rail left the station. While that would be a huge turn off to some, this was actually an attractive feature for her. It meant her clients would have an easy way to get to her. Ideally, she wouldn't usually advocate for girls taking the light rail alone, but some of her clients had no other options.

An alley separated the station from the property line of the houses on the block. She walked down the alley to stop in front of the property, noting that it had a garage. That was also a nice feature that some of the other houses they saw didn't have.

"The damage on the back of the house is pretty bad. I can take you through the garage, but I don't think it's safe to get too close," Sam said when Gianna finally joined them. "Any ideas what we can do with it, Hunter?"

"Let me get a closer look. I've got some ideas that I want to confirm."

Five minutes later, he returned to stand with them

in the alley.

"It's a salvageable disaster, as long as you have the time and money." Drawing on his background of architecture and urban design, he pictured what could be. "The basement was likely a studio apartment. I'd like to turn it into a one-bedroom unit. That's where the businesses would go."

"Businesses? More than one?" Gianna asked.

"Sure. Sam and Eliana have an office too, right? In my mind, there's no reason why you can't share the space. They could use it during the day, when kids are in school, and you use it in the evening when their business is closed. You would just have to work out a system for weekends."

"Damn," Eliana said. "Why didn't we think of that before?"

"It's a really good idea," Gianna murmured, impressed.

"Something to consider. For the rest, we take the four units and convert them into two semi-detached houses. The stairwells will be the shared walls, which will go a long way to ensuring quiet and privacy." He took a step back, looking down the alley again. "If we rebuild this three-car garage, we can probably build a studio apartment over it."

"Timeline?" Emilia asked.

He blew out a breath. "No less than nine months, but I would feel more comfortable saying a year. You have the district approvals to contend with and we're approaching the rainy season. If it's wet, we'll lose a lot of working days."

"Longer than we'd like," Emilia said quietly. "If we found something that wasn't falling down, it would be better."

"But isn't this what we've always wanted? Starting fresh completely. Making it our own from start to finish. Demo is practically done!" Sam cheered.

"I'm in. Hunter's vision is just incredible. And long term, one of the kids could move in the studio or basement when they're older!"

"I love that idea!" Ciara said excitedly.

"Wait, hold on. Shouldn't we think about this? See other properties?"

"We can still see the rest of the properties I have lined up," Sam took Emilia's hand. "But I really do think this is the one. Let's put in the offer and see what happens. We probably won't get a response until tomorrow night anyway. They'll want to use the entire weekend before they make a decision."

Gianna took her other hand. "Zia would love it. She would love the hustle and bustle of the city life. Taking quiet morning walks around the park. I can see her with us in this space, even though she can't be here. You know I'm right."

Eliana exhaled deeply. "We have got to talk them down on the price."

Sam grinned. "That I can do."

CHAPTER 9

After going back and forth a few times, their offer was accepted Tuesday afternoon. To celebrate, Gianna insisted that they go out for dinner. Feeling excited over soon being able to call downtown Sacramento home, she chose a restaurant for them accordingly.

Frank Fat's was a family owned and operated business that had been open since 1939. Located two blocks from the State's historic Capitol Building, it served decadent Chinese cuisine that was featured in the MICHELIN Guide. While she wasn't doing anything as grand as running a restaurant for over eighty years, Gianna hoped that they would see even a small amount of the success that Frank Fat had achieved since immigrating to the United States.

The restaurant walls, painted in a vibrant and bold red, towered almost two stories, creating a grand and illustrious feeling. A bench spanned the entire wall on one side of the space with tables and chairs in front. On the opposite side was the bar, which also took up most of that wall and provided bar seating for food and drinks.

Their waiter ushered them to their table, which was set up for five instead of four. Before Gianna could ask about it, Hunter appeared beside her.

"You made it," Sam beamed.

"I just had to get someone to close up for me," he explained, pulling out Gianna's chair for her. "Thanks for letting me crash your celebration."

"We've been searching for a month and a half and thanks to your help, we feel confident that we've made the right decision. You should be celebrating with us too," Emilia insisted and grinned at Gianna. "Right, Gianna?"

Gianna forced a smile. "Absolutely."

"Great." Hunter put his arm on the back of Gianna's chair and leaned in. "To add to the occasion, I brought a few drawings."

That got her attention and her smile brightened her face the way he hoped it would. Four sets of excited eyes focused on him, but he only met hers.

"Let's order first and then we can take a look."

Because of her excitement, she forgot to be on guard toward him. For the first time in months, Hunter felt like their relationship was as it had been before he hurt her. She joked with and teased him, touched his hand or leg whenever she laughed uncontrollably. When he finally retrieved his drawings from his messenger bag, she pressed close to him to look and make suggestions with her family.

In that moment, he felt like he was looking into his future. This was the life he wanted, with these people at this table. He just had to convince Gianna that she wanted the same.

Still high on excitement, Gianna stretched and patted her full belly as they stood to leave. "I'm stuffed and still I feel like I'm floating on cloud nine. I'm going to walk to the Capitol to see the tree and get some of this energy out."

Emilia led the way out. "We're taking Ciara on Saturday, or we would join you."

"I'll keep her company. Make sure she doesn't float away," Hunter added.

"Perfect," Emilia said with a grin.

Outside, they hugged and said goodbye before walking in opposite directions. The temperature had dropped dramatically now that the sun was down. Though they didn't get snow in Sacramento, nights like these often brought plenty of frost. She pulled on her gloves as she walked.

"I haven't seen the tree in years," Hunter shared as he zipped up his coat and pulled his hood over his head. "I forgot that they even did it."

"I try to stop by every year, but it's Emilia and Sam's Christmas tradition. They'll go see the tree and then drive through the Fab 40s to see the lights."

"You don't join them?"

"Sometimes I'll see the tree with them, but I don't like riding through the Fab 40s. It's too crowded."

The California Capitol Christmas Tree had been a holiday staple since 1931. Placed on the west lawn of Capitol Park, the tree stood at least sixty feet tall and was decorated in lights and beautiful handcrafted ornaments. The Capitol Dome glowed as if it served as the giant tree's topper. Though it was a Tuesday night, there was a small handful of people who had also come to take in the sight.

Hunter and Gianna stood shoulder to shoulder as they silently stared up at the tree. Behind them, the expanse of the Capitol Mall provided a clear and stunning view of the brightly lit Tower Bridge.

"Hunter," she sighed contentedly and leaned

against him. "Thank you. I know we still have a long way to go, but I'm already so grateful for what you've given us."

"You're welcome."

He put an arm around her shoulder to pull her closer. Her warmth spread through him. Her scent set the fire in his belly ablaze. Before he could stop himself, he turned both their bodies so that they were facing each other. The hand that was around her shoulder cupped the back of neck while his other fisted on the small of her back.

"Gianna," he whispered, drawing closer until their lips were inches apart.

"No," she whispered and put a hand between them.

Hunter sighed, but pulled back slightly. He moved his hand to cup her cheek and let his thumb brush over her lips.

"I'm sorry. It's just that these last few weeks…seeing you, touching you, smelling you, hearing you…I just have this burning need to satisfy the last sense with another taste."

Gianna knocked his hand away from her face with her left hand and landed a punch to his gut with her right. She took a step back and scowled at him.

"Why are men like this? You take kindness as interest and a smile as an invitation. You want, so you'll cajole and harass until you get it."

"You're right," he admitted, wincing in pain. He wasn't sure if his stomach or hand hurt more. Both had been powerful strikes, even at such a close distance. "I'm sorry."

"You *are* a sorry piece of—"

"That's true too," he interrupted and stepped closer to her. "I've been a sorry piece of shit ever since I let a bunch of bullies convince me that the girl I had a crush on was a whore who still couldn't possibly be interested in a socially awkward twig like me. I was a piece of shit for not standing up for you even when I knew it couldn't be true. It was easier to believe you were a whore than accept that I wasn't good enough for you."

Hunter sighed, wishing someone had given his teenage self the same treatment she had just given him.

"I'm definitely a sorry piece of shit, and have been to women for most of my life. Despite months and months of therapy trying to change this, I still hurt you by accusing you of being something you've never been. I'm sorry for it every damn day."

Gianna crossed her arms over her chest and looked away. "You clearly have a lot to unpack still. Between that and the upcoming renovations, the last thing you need to put your energy into is pursuing me."

Hunter stuck his hands in his pockets. "You asked why men are the way they are. Most of us are assholes or working not to be pieces of shits. In this case, however, it doesn't exactly apply."

She slanted a look at him. "What do you mean?"

Hunter grinned. "*Your* kindness *is* interest and your smile is an invitation. I sweet-talk and pursue you because we both want the same thing."

Gianna rubbed her temples. "It's like I'm trying to reason with brick wall."

"As a contractor, I like knocking down walls. The one you're trying to put up between us doesn't stand a chance."

Dropping her hands, she stared straight at him and enunciated each word as clearly as she could. "I don't like you. I don't want you. Please get that through your thick skull."

"How about this," he continued as if she hadn't spoken. "Let's take some time to really think about this. A month is your usual, right? We'll do the just friends thing. We chat, we play video games and stuff like that, just like before. I won't hit on you. If at the end of that month you're still letting yourself believe that there's nothing between us, then I'll back off."

He took his hands out of his pockets and extended his right hand toward her.

Gianna swatted his hand away. "I'm not negotiating with you. We were developing a good friendship, and I've hired you as a contractor. These are the only relationships I'm willing to entertain. You're the one in denial for thinking there is going to be something more between us. The sooner you accept that it's not going to happen, the better."

Hunter clucked his tongue. "Normally, I would believe you. I'll confess that I feel a seed of doubt sprouting, but then I remember that it was your sister who took the first swing at the wall before handing me the sledgehammer."

She scowled. "What the hell are you talking about?"

"Emilia told me everything," he confessed. "About those rumors in high school."

"That doesn't change anything for me," she said with a shrug, though her heart tripped with anxiety at the mention of the past. She was glad he knew, but she hated that Emilia had to rehash all of it to enlighten him.

"She also said that you had a crush on me. Not in high school. Right now."

Gianna gaped at him. "She did not!"

He laughed. "And since you like me, you'd try to

put up a wall between us. She doesn't want you to, not if you're doing it because of her and my own stupidity. That's why I said she took the first swing."

"You're both ridiculous," she said, frustrated.

"But is she wrong?"

"You're going to believe what you want anyway," she said with a shrug. "My answer doesn't matter."

She brushed past him to leave, and that had been a mistake. Standing out in the cold, with the Christmas tree glowing behind them, there was no lack of space and she could have moved by him without coming even an inch within his personal bubble. There were even less people than before, so it was utterly foolish to get so close to him. She basically stepped right into a hunting trap.

Hunter grabbed her hand and pulled her to him. With one hand fisted in her hair and the other holding her arm behind her back, he yanked her closer still and pressed his mouth to hers. All at once, his five senses were immersed in her and finally, *finally*, fully satisfied. Like a man starved for months, he devoured her in greedy gulps. He bit and tugged at her lips until she groaned in pain or pleasure. Or surrender.

There should have been fear. There should have been anger. If another man accosted her this way, no one would blame her for breaking his arm. Instead, there was only the startling gratification of surrender. It was such a pleasure to be kissed and held by him this way, to kiss him back with the same unrestrained passion that he showed her. When he tilted her head back and pulled away to let her breathe, she warred with the desire to push him away and pull him closer. In the end, she could only stare at him.

"Tell me she was wrong," he demanded. "I dare

you."

Gianna shook her head. "Let go. This is a mistake"

Frustrated, he resisted the need to kiss her again and prove her wrong. But he didn't dare loosen his hold, knowing she would bolt. Or worse, he thought wryly, remembering how she had just socked him.

"Why? This is the second time I've kissed you, Gianna. You responded in a way that proves there's something here. I want you. You want me. Why is this a mistake?"

"I already told you," she hissed, moving her free hand in between them. "Besides, look what happened the first time you started wanting more? Clearly friends are all we're meant to be."

"You keep speaking as if we can't be both. As if we can't have both friendship and more," he added in confusion. "Don't all relationships start as friendships before evolving into more? Isn't that what we've been doing, whether we were aware of it or not, since that first night we played games together?"

"And what about when it's over? When things fall apart? What happens to our friendship then?"

Baffled, he gentled his hold, but kept her body pressed against his just in case she decided to lash out. He stroked her lower back lightly and cupped the back of her head.

"You're already ending it when it's only just beginning. I didn't know you were such a pessimist."

Gianna shoved him away. "I'm a realist. This isn't happening. If you keep pushing me, we won't even be friends."

"Wait," he insisted when she stormed away. "Let me at least walk you to the garage."

Ignoring him, she kept walking. It was probably

best that he followed her. If someone did attack her, she wasn't sure she wouldn't take all her anger out on them and accidently commit murder.

She knew the anger was a cover, but refused to think beyond it. If he wouldn't protect their friendship, then she would do it all by herself.

She just had to keep pretending that she wasn't already falling for him.

∞∞∞∞∞∞

"Kudos for not murdering my cousin," Valerie grinned as she refilled their glasses.

Scowling, Gianna eyed the glass as she waited. "There's still time."

London chuckled. "It's been two weeks. Why are you still so mad?"

"Because any minute, his dumb face is going to walk in here and probably ruin another good night." Pleasantly buzzed, Gianna sipped more wine. "He's so hard headed. I don't trust him not to try something."

"It's about time, if you ask me," London said, also inebriated. "I can't believe it took me so long to realize that his hate for you was really just a mask for his crush. It's classic dumb boy behavior."

"Fuck 'em!" Gianna yelled.

"Isn't that his goal? And yours too?" London teased. "Your panties are still on fire from that kiss!"

"You and Emilia are both good for nothing traitors!" She threw her arm around Valerie's shoulder. "You're the only one who is on my side, Val. The only one I trust. Why aren't you more drunk? It's your house! You've got no excuse."

"It's a lot of work to host a New Year's Eve party," she confessed, moving her hand around Gianna's waist. "I have to stay relatively sober to keep the party going."

"Less hosting and more toasting!" Gianna held up her glass.

Valerie laughed and tapped her glass against Gianna's before taking a sip. "A toast to your first real relationship."

Gianna groaned and tried pulling away. "Not you too! Why won't anyone listen to me?"

"We are listening," London said. She moved to Gianna's opposite side and also put her arm around her waist. "We hear the words you aren't saying. Hunter has always meant a lot to you. You're so good at cutting people out of your life, so you're afraid you'll have to cut him out if this relationship doesn't work out."

Valerie leaned her head against Gianna's. "There are no guarantees. It's all a risk. You know London and I speak with scarred experience. We know it's terrifying to willingly open yourself up to those risks. We also know that it was worth it."

"Maybe he couldn't handle a friendship and more back in high school, but you're both all grown up now. And he won't be like the other men you see who are happy to have you for a few nights before you ghost them. Hunter isn't built like that," London assured her.

"All the more reason for him to look for someone who actually has relationship experience. Who is actually relationship material. Ow!"

London pinched her ass again. "Don't belittle my friend like that."

"You've been the glue in this trio from the start,"

Valerie reminded her. "That's damn near twenty years of relationship experience. You got this."

Gianna pouted. "Let me just have one more night of being in denial. One more night before everything changes."

"Alright," London soothed and also pressed her head against Gianna's. "One more night."

They created quite the image for Hunter when he finally walked in. Three gorgeous women, each dressed in a dazzling sequined gown, holding each other up and together in front of the crackling fire. There was nothing more beautiful than the friendship they had nurtured. Though he suspected, and hated, that his behavior continued to cause Gianna some discomfort, he would forever be grateful to the two women that embraced her with the love he wanted to give her.

Hunter shook his head, deciding that he definitely needed to throw back a few bottles of water before he spoke to Gianna. She didn't need any more reasons to run from him.

Though it was a struggle to tear his gaze from her, Hunter managed to focus on removing his shoes without falling over before he entered the house. The men came stumbling out of the kitchen as he approached, laughing raucously at some joke.

"There he is!" Jun shouted, as he made his way over. "You just missed the cigars. What took you so long? It's already 9:30."

Hunter accepted the drunken hug and nearly toppled over. "The guys from work were pissed that I haven't hung out with them as much as I planned this year. They kept sending shots my way knowing I was ditching them for you all."

"Guess they can't know that you've got something

much more important going on over here," Tony said with a grin as his gaze swung over to Gianna. "Need a drink?"

"Water, please. I was in danger of puking in the ride share."

He had missed most of the people and the party while he was out bar hopping with Todd. After he filled a plate with food, he kept Jun and Valerie company while they tidied the kitchen. The others retreated into the living room for party games. Since he wanted to sober up, he didn't press Gianna after she barely greeted him.

It was probably for the best. He remembered all too clearly their last encounter and was hungry for another taste. Added to that, he received an arousing surprise when he observed her from his seat at the counter. Though the bold blue sequined dress had long sleeves, there was no fabric on the back. The dress dipped low, flirting at the top of the waist and creating a canvas of bare skin. Between that and its mid-thigh length, he found his mouth watering and his fingers itching to touch all that tantalizing skin.

It was going to be extremely difficult to be on his best behavior tonight.

Thankfully, two and a half hours flew by. He managed, just barely, to keep his hands to himself, but he was certain that everyone in the room caught him watching Gianna with hungry eyes. Though he was no longer drunk, he had enough of a buzz that he didn't feel any of the shame that he probably should. The men had already called him out at the Kings game and he knew Gianna had already told her friends what happened. How he felt and what he wanted wasn't a secret anymore anyway.

A few minutes till midnight, they gathered in front of the TV and passed around confetti poppers and noise makers. With the TV turned on to the Time Square Ball Drop, Hunter again noticed that everyone was paired up except for him and Gianna. He never cared about the traditional New Year's Eve kiss before, but he would take any excuse to kiss her right now.

Hunter leaned against the pony wall separating the family and sitting room, prepared to bolt the moment the others started locking lips. He had enough torture for one night.

At the one-minute mark, London and Valerie once again surrounded Gianna.

"Okay, so you've had your one night. Go lay one on that dummy and give us some fireworks," London insisted as she gave Gianna a little shove.

"Hey!" Gianna refused to budge. "It's still the same night!"

"Is it though?" Valerie asked. "The new year is in thirty seconds. That's a new night to me."

"Literally a new year," London clarified and gave her a harder shove. "Go take a risk, scaredy cat."

"Cat? More like chicken," Valerie teased and pushed her toward Hunter.

Before she could voice her anger, the others set off their poppers. Shouts and cheers rang in the new year before quickly giving way to silence as the couples embraced. Kissed.

"Gawd fucking damn it!" She scowled. "Fuck it, then."

Hunter had already pushed away from the wall and was turning towards the kitchen when Gianna caught his hand to stop him. Her other hand looped around his neck to pull him down. Standing on her toes, she met him halfway.

It started as just a press of lips against lips. Simple, chaste, innocent. But she heard his sharp intake of breath, saw the way his eyes flew open in surprise. For some reason, his reaction spurred her on and she deepened the kiss. Changed the angle, lips moving actively against his as he kissed her back.

But the moment she felt him reach for her, panic seized her chest and she quickly released him. Before he could speak, she bolted from the room.

Stunned, aroused, Hunter moved to sit in one of the barstools at the counter. He sipped his water and stared past the kitchen where she had gone while he willed himself to stay exactly where he was. It was the first time she initiated anything between them and probably did so because she was drunk and caught up in the moment. The last thing he needed to do was make that inch into a mile when she didn't even mean it. He had taken too many liberties with her already.

"Happy New Year!" Valerie said, jolting him from his thoughts as she threw her arm around him. "I think it'll be a good one for you and Gianna. Wait, where's Gianna?"

Hunter took a big gulp of water. "Sick maybe? She ran into bathroom."

"On no! How could she be sick? She hasn't had a drink since like ten." Concerned, Valerie called to her friend as she approached the bathroom.

Valerie's words echoed through his mind, drowning out every reason he had concocted for remaining exactly where he was now. She wasn't drunk, and though he wasn't either, he felt anything but sober as he stood to his feet and marched across the room. He wouldn't wait any longer. Couldn't possibly wait any longer.

Inside the bathroom, Gianna leaned against the sink with her back to the mirror and tried to calm her racing heart and douse the inferno that threatened to consume her. It had been foolish to continue to deny that she wanted him for this long anyway, but she wasn't expecting to feel so overwhelmed with desire after another kiss. It was like each time they touched, each time they kissed, she needed and wanted more. If they weren't careful, they would burn each other up and leave nothing behind.

Knowing she couldn't hide from him forever, she turned to rinse her hands with cold water as if that would help her feel better.

"Gianna? Are you okay?" Valerie asked after knocking lightly on the door.

"I'm fine," she responded shakily and turned the water off. "Coming out now."

She dried her hands and unlocked the door. She was opening it when she heard Valerie shout.

"Hey! Excuse you!"

Gianna looked up just as Hunter pushed his way in front of Valerie. He filled the doorway and just kept moving, forcing her to step back until she hit the vanity. She registered the sound of the door slamming shut and the lock turning. She wasn't sure who reached for who first, but his arms came around her to lift her onto the sink.

With their bodies pressed closely together, she gave herself to the kiss. His mouth was greedy and demanding as it moved against hers, forcing her to race to keep up with his impatient pace. His hands, hot and calloused, moved up her back, and made her feel just as impatient. With desperation seeping through her pores, she wrapped her legs around his waist to bring him closer still.

In response, Hunter slid his hand down her back, over her hip and down that long, bare leg just like he imagined doing all night. Her dress, already short, inched up further to accommodate her movements, and left, he discovered as he palmed her, her bare ass exposed.

Speechless, he fisted his hand in her hair and tugged her head back, breaking the kiss. If she was completely naked under this dress, he would absolutely lose his shit and take her right there on his cousin's vanity.

"Are you...?" He brushed his fingers upward and felt the thin fabric of her thong. He was both relieved and devastated to discover that she was in fact wearing underwear.

Gianna chuckled. "Of course not, you degenerate. There's a bra and a thong under here."

"How? Never mind. Doesn't matter." He shook his head, intending to find out on his own. "Come home with me."

She really, really wanted to. If he was any other man, she would have. She would have allowed herself a few hours of pleasure and then return home, content and satisfied. After three or four times, she would end it and move on.

But this was Hunter, and she valued what they had more than she was willing to admit. In some ways, she felt they were moving too fast. In others, the pace was slow. She hoped to get a handle on her emotions before she took things to the next level.

So, reluctantly, she placed her hands on his chest and gave him a light push so she could get down. Thankfully, he released her, though he didn't give her much space. She pulled her dress down and then shook out her hair.

"We really shouldn't. We've both had a lot to drink tonight, and I'm staying here tonight for that very reason."

Her response hit him like a bucket of ice-cold water, effectively quenching his desire. Staggered by the abrupt shift from hot to cold, Hunter took a step back. They were both sober, but even after that kiss they shared, she still pushed him away. He released a tired sigh. He actually felt the familiar exhaustion of swinging a sledgehammer. How foolish of him to think he had successfully knocked down her walls when he had barely made a dent. He was so fucking tired.

"Fine," he said quietly as he turned to unlock the door. He stepped to the side to open it and avoided looking at her.

"Hunter," she said, sensing something was wrong. "Please don't misunderstand, I—"

"I understand," he said and pushed her out of the bathroom. "It's fine."

Gianna frowned at the door after he closed it, certain that he misunderstood. Since she heard him actually using the bathroom, she decided to drop it for the moment. She would clear it up before he left.

The moment she stepped into the kitchen, Valerie pounced.

"That was fast," she said with a grin.

Gianna snorted. "I don't think Jun would appreciate us doing the deed on his vanity, so, shockingly, we managed to keep it PG-13."

"Sounded more like NC-17."

Gianna blushed. "You were *not* seriously listening, were you?"

"Not the whole time," she laughed. "London pulled me away. So, are you leaving with him?"

"He asked, but I said we shouldn't, and now I'm worried he misunderstood that to mean not ever."

As soon as she said it, he came out of the bathroom. He looked calm, but she got the distinct sense that he was far from it. Though he had done a piss poor job of pretending that he hadn't been checking her out all night, he walked through the kitchen and to the living room without so much as glancing at her.

Valerie raised an eyebrow as she watched him go. "Definitely misunderstood."

"Fucking hell," she sighed. She made her way into the living room to see him walking out the door. "Where's he going?"

London looked up from the couch where she was snuggled up next to Tony. "Next door to get an energy drink from Ruben so he can drive home. I haven't seen him look that grumpy since college."

"Gawd fucking damn it!" Gianna shouted and raced upstairs.

London perked up when she came back down with her duffle bag. "Yes, girl! Go get some New Years Day Dick!"

Gianna laughed breathlessly as she rushed to the door. "You're a mess."

"I'll text you where to meet for lunch tomorrow so you can tell us all about it," London winked at her.

Gianna didn't bother protesting. She quickly slipped on her boots, picked up her jacket, and darted out the door. The cold made her nearly squeal, and she pulled on her jacket as she walked to the street. She hadn't realized it when she arrived earlier that day, but Hunter had left his truck here and taken a ride share downtown to drink with his friends. She saw it now that the street was empty but for his, Tony, and her car.

Hunter was about to cross the street when she called to him. He stopped and turned to stare at her when she rushed over to him.

"What are you doing?"

She held up her hand for a second as she caught her breath. "You misunderstood."

"Since when does no not mean no, Gianna?" He asked, unable to keep the anger out of the voice.

"I didn't say no. I said we shouldn't, but I didn't say no. I just…fuck. I really have no fucking clue how to do this. I want to be with you tonight, but—"

"No buts," he interrupted. "Yes or no, Gianna."

"Yes," she grabbed his hand. "Hunter. Yes, I will go home with you."

CHAPTER 10

His hands were shaking on the steering wheel as he drove home, keeping his speed low so she could follow him. He could have given her his address, but a part of him was worried she would change her mind and keep on driving. Somehow, being able to peek at her through his rear-view window made him feel a little more secure.

His phone rang and his heart sunk when he saw her name flash across his dashboard screen, thinking she might back out. Forcing himself not to panic, he took a breath before he answered.

"Hello?"

"I should explain some things before…I need you to understand where I'm coming from and why I've been hesitant about all of this."

"Okay," he said, wondering where this was going. What more could there be outside of what Emilia had told him?

Gianna sighed. "I don't…I haven't…I've never been in a relationship before."

Hunter blinked, utterly confused. "You're a virgin?"

"What?" She laughed, and would have kept laughing if she wasn't driving. "No! Oh, my god. As if.

I've never been in a serious, long-term relationship. The boyfriend, girlfriend thing? I've never done it."

"Seriously?"

"Seriously. I know Emilia told you about our DNA providers, about how she dealt with it all. Of course it fucked me up too, but in a different way. Compound that with my high school experience with boys and being sexually assaulted in college and you've got this beautiful mess that is Gianna. Despite years of therapy, I haven't managed to fully unfuck my complicated feelings about men and relationships."

Hunter slowed as it started to rain and also because he needed to process this confession without driving off the road.

"You just breezed through all of that as if it's no big deal. It's all a big deal." His hands tightened on the steering wheel as if they were around the neck of whoever dared hurt her. "You were assaulted."

"One in three women are sexually assaulted at least once in their lifetime. That statistic has largely remained unchanged since I was a kid. It is a big deal, but it's also an unfortunate and somewhat normalized reality for women. We live our lives expecting it to happen, surviving it after the fact, or both. This life comes to us as naturally as breathing."

"That's fucking awful."

"That's life as a woman," she sighed ruefully. "Lucky for me, a woman who trained in jiu-jitsu intervened before things got bad. But, as you can imagine, being grabbed and groped from behind was still traumatizing and it took a few years in therapy and in martial arts for me to feel like I could function normally in public again."

"Gianna," he whispered, realizing how many times

he had likely inadvertently triggered her trauma.

"Anyway," she said cheerfully to change the mood, knowing full well where his thoughts had headed. "I brought all this up so that you understand that this is new territory for me. Friendships are all I know, and even that circle is really small. In many ways, the adult Gianna became that flirt those high schoolers accused me of being, but I have always been very selective about who actually gets to have me. I've only gotten to know a man long enough to ensure he won't murder or assault me, and then I quickly got out just in case he was just biding his time. Walking away is easier for me than maintaining the relationship once intimacy becomes the center of it. I don't want to do that with you."

"That's why you've insisted that we're only friends."

"I come with a lot of baggage, and only some of it would touch you if we're just friends. But what we're about to do... You sure you want to deal with all of it?"

"I'm grateful that you trust me enough to share this. I have my own baggage too," he answered honestly. "I want you, so we'll deal with it together. You want me enough to try something that makes you uncomfortable so I'll do everything in my power to make sure you always feel safe with me."

"I've always felt safe with you," she said quietly.

"Even when I grabbed you from behind? You were trembling. At the time, I didn't think it was from fear."

She shifted in her seat, remembering how it felt. "It wasn't."

"What was that?"

"You heard me. Asshole."

Hunter chuckled. "I never did give you your reward for being such a good girl."

"You're ridiculous."

"I've had a lot of time to think about it, but I'm curious. What kind of reward would you like?"

A few erotic images flitted through her mind. She squeezed her thighs together in anticipation.

"We can discuss my reward in your bed."

"I like the sound of that," he said quietly. "Drive carefully. It's wet out now."

"It's not hard to drive in the rain."

"It's very hard. Especially with your voice in my ears."

She bit her lip. "Why are you driving so slow?"

"I like to go slow."

"I like to go fast."

"I'll change that."

"Are we almost there?"

"Are you? Well?" he asked when she didn't respond. "No answer? That's okay. I think I'll touch you there first to find out for myself."

"I'm hanging up now!"

His rumbling laughter was the last thing she heard before she hung up. It was really quite pathetic how easily that man riled her up. A few sensual words had butterflies dancing in her stomach. After she finally parked in front of his house, her heart practically exploded from her chest when she saw him walking toward her car.

Hunter tossed his jacket over her the moment she climbed from the car. Ignoring her protests, he kept her protected from the rain as he escorted her inside. He laughed when she threw herself into his arms the moment they crossed the threshold.

"Slow down," he insisted.

"No. Hurry up."

Gianna dropped her bag, kicked her shoes off and peeled off her coat off all-in-one go. Impressed, he responded simply by lifting her into his arms. After toeing off his own shoes, he carried her to his room and tossed her on his bed.

"Wait here. Stay dressed."

"What? Why? Where are you——?"

He was gone before she could finish, leaving her in the dark. Light from the hallway filtered in through the door, but it wasn't enough for her to make out much of the room itself. Thankfully, he returned a few moments later with her bag, now overflowing with candles.

"Hunter, this is completely unnecessary," she said as he went about the room placing and lighting candles of all sizes. The soft, flickering flames created a sensual and romantic glow.

Ignoring her, Hunter opened one of his windows so the sound of rain filled the silence. Then he turned to face her and watched her as he began to undress.

"Hey, let me," she said, rising to her knees to get up.

"Don't move."

Gianna glared at him. "You're bossy. It's annoying."

"And yet, you're so very obedient," he said with a grin and stepped out of his pants. He left his boxers on for the moment and crossed to the bed. "Lie back."

She turned her nose up at him, refusing to move.

"This works too," he said.

With one hand speared in her hair and another on her waist, Hunter yanked her up and against him. Since she had been expecting him to push her back against the bed, she wasn't prepared to resist. Defeat never tasted this good, she thought, moaning against him as he kissed her.

Though his lips moved roughly against hers, he kept the pace achingly slow. With a fistful of her hair, he pulled her back each time she tried to speed up and instead pressed his lips against her neck. The contrast was devastating. Desperate, she stuck her hand in his boxers to show him that she wanted more.

She nearly wept in gratitude when his hands cupped her ass to lift her. *Finally*, she thought, and wrapped her legs around his waist as he laid her back against the bed. The relief was brief as he merely went back to kissing her slowly, his hand lazily dancing down her body until it found its way between her legs.

"So wet," he whispered as he toyed with her over her panties. "Roll over. Show me that back that taunted me all night."

"More commands? We have got to break this bad habit of yours."

He slipped a finger inside. "Roll. Over."

She obeyed with a small moan.

"Good girl. Here's your reward."

He added another finger, but didn't change his pace. Kisses trailed across her back, matching the slow movements of his fingers. If she dared move her hips to increase the pace, he merely stopped his movements until she settled down again. A powerful orgasm built and built, but every time she tried to sprint towards the finish line, he dragged her back by stopping his ministrations.

"Hunter, please," she begged.

He sighed against her, content to carry on this way even though his cock throbbed painfully.

"Tell me what you want."

Gianna pushed weakly to her hands and knees. She

managed to peel off her panties before she straddled him.

"Let me get a condom."

"Not yet," she said and moved her way up his body until she sat on his face.

He didn't go slow this time. Couldn't even if he wanted to. Happy to let her take control here, he licked and sucked her clit, keeping the mad pace of her hips as she rocked and bucked against his mouth. Wanting to feast on her all night, he ate and ate and ate until she came.

With her taste filling his body, the last strings on his control finally snapped. He pushed her roughly onto her back and sat up to retrieve a condom from his night stand.

"Take off your dress. Hurry up," he demanded, ripping the package open.

He moved faster than she could. Still trembling from her orgasm, Gianna could do little more than release her arms from the dress. Impatient, Hunter grabbed her ankle and pulled her to the edge of the bed. The moment he climbed on top of her, he slammed inside of her, filling her completely.

Gone was the gentle, slow lover. Here was the hunter, mad with desire and starved of pleasure. Eager to take his prey, his movements were wild and rough. Sometimes he held one of her legs up while other times his hand dug into her hips, but his pace never slowed.

"Take it off," he demanded.

Here was the aggressive, domineering man Gianna had come to expect. He barely slowed as she tugged and pulled, wiggled and squirmed until she had the dress off. And still she wanted more. She moaned his name, begging for it. *More*, she thought, her mind reeling from the realization. When he finally came and collapsed on top of her, she still wanted more.

She wanted more, and for the first time, she was certain that more didn't have a limit.

With his face buried against her neck, Hunter inhaled her scent as he caught his breath. Gathering his strength, he flipped onto his back, and with her still in his arms, managed to worm his way into the center of his bed. The comforter had been knocked askew just enough for him to pull at it until it covered them.

Not knowing what else to do, Gianna let herself be held. With her head pressed against his chest to hear the steady beating of his heart, she smiled as he gently stroked her hair.

"Oh, so you can be gentle."

Hunter chuckled. "I'm full of surprises. Go to sleep and I'll wake you up with one."

"Pervert," she accused, but she settled in and closed her eyes. She still felt pretty wired, but between the scent of the candles, the warmth of his body, and his gentle touch, she was out within minutes.

Hunter, however, remained wide awake. When he was certain she was out, he slowly and carefully slipped from the bed. Though his body was fully satisfied, his mind was still grappling with her confession. And planning how to use it his advantage.

Gianna had never been in a real relationship before, and that would work out in his favor. He would raise the bar so high that should he somehow manage to fuck this up, any man that came after him would never be able to reach it and would forever be standing in Hunter's shadow.

Before he could go bed, he had to set his plan in motion to be the first and only love Gianna ever had.

∞∞∞∞∞∞

Gianna heard the soft patter of rain as she began to wake. If not for the bright sunlight that streamed into the room, she could have easily buried back into Hunter's warmth and drifted back to sleep. But now her brain was awake. Half draped over his body, she let her thoughts spin as she processed her feelings.

Waking in the arms of her lover was another first for her. Of course, there was a small handful of times where she stayed the night with a man she had vetted enough to warrant a repeat session, but she had never shown or expected to receive any sort of affection. The lazy way Hunter brushed her hair or stroked her back as she lay there made her heart stir.

Although his passion bordered on rough, she found herself enjoying their little power struggles. She never thought she could be a sub, but there was something about giving in to Hunter that was sexy and thrilling. The contrast of his current behavior, however, was another story. This gentleness was a well-aimed arrow that struck her heart dead center. She was certain his duality would be her undoing.

"I didn't expect you to be a cuddler," he said suddenly, his deep voice just above a whisper.

"I'm not. It's just freezing in here. Why didn't you close the window last night? Hell, why did you even open it?"

Gianna tilted her head to look at him. He put his phone down to brush a finger over her lips before leaning down to kiss her.

"I'll close it now," he said, doubting she would be pleased to learn that he had done it to ensure she would cling to him all night. He slipped from the bed to cross the room. "There's a glass of water for you. Coffee should be done brewing too. Do you want any?"

"I'll get it," she said, sitting up to stretch.

Her hair tumbled messily around her shoulders and caressed the swell of her breasts. She created quite the image, stirring his heart with need. He wanted to keep her there, looking just like that, a bit longer.

"No. Stay there," he demanded and left before she could object.

Gianna snorted and got up. "I take back my thoughts about being a sub. Can't do it. I just can't!"

He returned just as she was pulling a sweatshirt over her head.

"Get back in bed or you won't get your reward."

She yanked the sweatshirt down and turned to yell at him. "Listen, I don't—Are those donuts? When did you get donuts?"

A white bag with a signature pink donut box inside hung from his arm. He carried a large piece of wood, using it in lieu of a tray. On it was a pot of coffee, mugs, sugar, and creamer.

"Back in bed first."

They stared at each other. She didn't want to cave, but damn it, the man didn't play fair. How the hell was she supposed to resist donuts and coffee in bed? When he grinned at her like he knew exactly what she was thinking, she flipped him off before getting back into bed.

"If you say good girl, I swear I'll put you in a headlock."

"With your thighs?" He asked as he brought over

the makeshift tray and set it on the night stand closest to her. "Didn't you do that this morning?"

Ignoring him, she poured them both a cup of coffee. He opened the bag and box and offered her a glazed donut.

"You woke up shortly after the donuts got delivered."

"Makes sense. My body craves buttery goodness," she confessed and took a bite.

Hunter titled his head in thought. "Did you just quote Burton Guster?"

Her mouth twitched in amusement before she quoted him again. "You know that's right."

"You and you are a one hundred percent match from your personality questionnaires," he thought, recalling another line from the television show *Psych* as he stared at her.

Hunter cleared his throat and then he dug in his pocket to retrieve her phone. "We'll have to rewatch it together one day. You left it in the kitchen and it has been going off all morning," he explained.

She took another donut and her phone. "Probably London and Valerie telling me when and where to meet them so I can report back."

"Report back? On what?"

"This," she said, moving the donut between the two of them before she took a bite. "They'll want to hear all about it."

Hunter blinked. "Are you serious?"

"Yep. I'll have to relay every detail. I especially can't wait to tell them about every delicious inch of your rather large and impressive—"

Hunter covered her mouth. "You know, I'd rather my cousin and play sister not know about my anatomy."

"Sorry. It can't be helped," she said after pulling away. "I kind of started this whole thing so I definitely can't get out of it."

"And I thought men were bad. Well, I guess I should give you something else to talk about."

Gianna grinned as he pushed her back against the bed, covered her body with his, and gave her much more to say.

CHAPTER 11

"How did we end up helping you pack when we only came to hear about your dirty deeds? You're not moving for months!"

Gianna handed London a roll of tape. "You both have insisted, repeatedly I might add, that you would help me pack. Not only did I take you up on that offer, I told you everything and bought lunch! Really, you're getting the better end of the deal!"

"Not as good as the deal you had this morning. Donuts, coffee, and sex," London said.

"Oh my," Valerie sang.

"I guess I have been spoiled today. I still can't believe he did all of that," Gianna said, smiling in thought. "The sex alone was just…whew, incredible. After the dry spell I had, I feel like a changed woman. New dick, new me!"

London laughed. "Oh gawd, you're so crass."

"Gianna and Hunter," Valerie said thoughtfully. "It's weird, but also not? Or maybe it's weird because it seems right. Like it totally makes sense that the two of you are together."

"It *does* feel right and that *is* weird," Gianna confessed. "Being friends with him again was an easy transition because we have so much in common. I thought things would be a little awkward after sleeping together, but it wasn't. It was just…the same, but different. I know that doesn't make any sense."

Valerie smiled in understanding. "It does make sense."

"Gianna's got a boyfriend," London declared.

She put together another box, frowning. "We're not there yet. We didn't even talk about it actually, not in depth. I wouldn't be surprised if he feels weirded out about this being my first relationship now that he's had a chance to calm his raging hormones."

"If you're calling it your first relationship, how is he not your boyfriend?" London asked. "Don't minimize it just because the newness of it all makes you uncomfortable."

"Be honest," Valerie encouraged. "How are you feeling about things now?"

Gianna sighed and scooped up Fiona to snuggle. "Anxious. Excited. Hopeful. Desired. Needy. I'm a mess. This can't be normal."

Valerie slanted London a knowing look. A mutual thought passed between them and they both shook their heads, recognizing that speaking on it wouldn't help.

"I wouldn't worry about it too much," Valerie encouraged. "Just try to enjoy being with him for now."

"Besides, Hunter's a pretty steady guy. When I think about it, the only time I've ever seen him trip up is with you."

Gianna couldn't help but smile. She put Fiona down and went back to packing. "That's pretty cute."

"You're pretty cute," London said. "You're

practically glowing."

Gianna merely grinned because that was exactly how she felt. "I can't figure out if I'll see him more or less because of the work he'll be doing on the house."

Valerie taped up her own box. "You're going to make yourself crazy trying to figure it all out right now. You've already got a lot to deal with. Packing, getting this place sold, moving."

"Are Fiona and Shrek going to stay with you at Emilia's?" London asked.

"Yeah, but I actually want to move them sooner. I don't want to have to crate them every time there's a showing so I'm trying to figure that out. I still want to be able to see and spend time with them. I could take them to Emilia's now, but that would put me at her house more often. I'm not ready to have us all squeezed in to her place that often so early in the renovations. Anyway, I'll make it work somehow. We aren't planning to put this place on the market until March at the earliest. And even that will depend on whether or not we're able to stay on budget."

They continued to pack as they offered her suggestion and ideas. As the day progressed, their conversations meandered between the men in their lives, to work, and everything else that was going on. She updated them on her progress on creating and finding donors for the STEM scholarship through her non-profit before they made their way home.

Alone, she took stock of her condo. They had packed up nearly all of her gaming, anime, and TV collectibles and memorabilia in the second bedroom and staged it to look like any other office. The boxes they filled were moved to the garage where she would eventually reorganize to fit more boxes and items she removed from inside.

Though it was only five, her body finally registered the sheer exhaustion of the last twenty for hours. Ready for bed, she showered and changed into her pajamas. When she came out to make dinner, she found Shrek and Fiona waiting impatiently for their wet food. After feeding them, she carried her own leftovers from lunch to the couch to watch a show.

Halfway through it, her phone rang.

"Hey, Hunter," she answered, unable to keep the grin from her face.

"Hey. You better not be watching *Psych* without me," he said.

Gianna shook her head. "If you're going to stalk my status on the PlayStation, I'm going to report you."

"Damn, I was just curious. I wanted to play Vault Hunters, but I'm doing a belated New Years Day breakfast with my family tomorrow morning."

"Maybe tomorrow night then," she suggested, petting Shrek after he made his way into her lap.

"I was hoping to play something else tomorrow. Let me take you out to dinner," he said.

"Another demand."

Hunter grinned. "Is that what that was?"

"Well, it certainly wasn't a question," she said mockingly.

"Then that means I'll see you tomorrow. Tell me what time you're free and I'll figure the rest out."

"Hunter," she sighed loudly, unsure if she was annoyed or aroused. "Try again."

"Hmmm, I don't think so," he said thoughtfully. "I do have a different question though."

"I'm dying to hear it."

"When are you going to let me taste you again?"

Definitely aroused, she thought as she closed her eyes.

"Say 'tomorrow,' Gianna," Hunted demanded.

"Tomorrow."

"Good girl."

∞∞∞∞∞∞

Hunter loved when a plan came together.

While Gianna had been sleeping in his arms New Years morning, he had been browsing dealerships on his phone. Before the accident, he preferred having a separate car for work that could haul all of the equipment and materials and one for personal use. It was his personal vehicle that had been totaled, and while he had every intention of replacing it, he never mustered the motivation to follow through.

Now, over a year since the accident, he couldn't put it off any longer. The inside of his work truck was an embarrassment, with its stained seats, assortment of empty food wrappers and bottles, tools, and left over materials. Even if he cleaned it, it would only be a matter of days before it returned to a disastrous state. It was much easier to bite the bullet and finally buy the car he had been saving for. So, while Gianna had been giving Valerie and London way more details than they deserved, he spent his day on the car lot.

Now Gianna could be the passenger princess she deserved to be and he received a great New Years deal on the car he had been eyeing for months.

Hunter pushed the speed limited a bit as he drove, testing out his new car, but also excited to see her again. He would have understood if she had been unwilling to see him again so soon. Being in a relationship was new territory for her so he worried that she would want to keep a little distance at first. Thankfully, that wasn't the case.

He needed to see her. Wanted another night to touch and taste. Just thinking about having her under him again made his hands tighten on the steering wheel. But more than that, he needed to keep getting in her way just like Emilia said. He wanted to show her that taking a chance on being in a relationship with him would be the most rewarding, most pleasurable experience of her life.

He could only hope that his plan to make her fall in love with him would be successful as well.

Hunter followed her directions for parking and walking to her condo. He knocked on her door and waited patiently.

"Hey, Hun—"

Gianna stopped midsentence when she saw the colorful bouquet of flowers Hunter held in his arms. An unfamiliar feeling danced in her stomach and chest. Part surprise, she was certain, but what was this other feeling?

"They're beautiful," she said quietly, a little breathless as she accepted the flowers. "Come in."

Feeling like she was in a scene from some rom-com, she led him inside and went to her kitchen to find a vase. Fiona, who was sitting by the water bowl beneath the peninsula, hissed as Hunter approached. Unperturbed, Hunter retrieved a cat treat from his pocket and bent down. With his palm open, he waited patiently for Fiona to approach.

Gianna stared at him curiously. "You came prepared."

Hunter shot her a grin as he offered Fiona another treat. "The flowers were just a ploy to get in your house so I could play with your pussy. Where's the other one?"

Shrek approached cautiously. Scenting treats, he mewled for his own and was quickly rewarded when Hunter held out his other hand. Her heart tripped a little at the sight. She didn't often have people over so both cats were usually wary of people in general, but especially men because she never had them over. But Hunter seemed to have won them over rather quickly.

"You know, when you said you wanted to play, this isn't what I was thinking," she said with a forced frown.

"Sorry," he said with a sheepish grin. "I've wanted to meet them since you told me about them. Who is who?"

"The white one is Fiona and the brown one is Shrek. I didn't know you liked cats."

Realizing that he was in fact worth her time, Fiona graciously offered her body for pets and scritches. Hunter was eager to oblige.

"I've always wanted a cat. Unfortunately, my parents and most of my siblings hate them so it never happened. I'd feel guilty about getting one now because I'm gone so much because of work."

"Why do you think I have two? They keep each other company when I can't."

"Hmm. I never thought of that," he said, standing to finally look around. "Nice place. Makes me want to stay here and watch *Psych* instead of going out for dinner."

"We could do that after dinner," she suggested.

"You sure? I wasn't fishing for an invitation."

"Oh?" Gianna picked up the coat and purse she had

left on the table. "I assumed you would get all bossy and tell me to tell you to let you stay."

Hunter followed her to the door. "I'm feeling a little more clearheaded and diplomatic now that I no longer have blue balls. I won't push you to do something you're not comfortable with."

"Somehow, I don't believe you," she replied honestly, locking the door after they stepped outside.

When she turned, she bumped right into him. Hunter placed his hands on her hips and leaned down to kiss her. Gentle, slow. Soft and agonizing, his lips gave new life to that strange feeling in her stomach where it settled comfortably beside the desire now burning in her gut. Suddenly, she didn't want to leave. She wanted to go back inside, take this man to bed where he would stroke and make her purr, and help her figure out what this feeling was.

She pulled away, pleaded. "Let's go back inside."

"Yes," he said roughly, his hands tightening briefly on her hips. "Wait. No. This is exactly why I didn't kiss you in there. I'm taking you on a proper date first."

Gathering his strength, he took her hand and led her to his car.

"I'm uncomfortable having dinner while I'm thinking about riding you," she confessed once they reached the parking lot. "You don't want to push me to do something uncomfortable, right?"

Hunter nearly lost his footing when he stepped off the curb. He managed to catch himself on his car, leaving a large handprint on the passenger window.

"Gianna," he said darkly, his voice full of warning.

"Hey, those were your words, not mine. Wait. Did you finally buy a new car?" she asked when he opened the door to a vehicle she had never seen before and that familiar new car smell wafted out to her.

"Yes," he answered, waiting for her to climb inside.

She didn't. Instead, she titled her head to stare at him in confusion. "What happened to your truck?"

"Nothing. I still have it. I prefer to have two cars and I've been eyeing this since the accident. There was a good sale yesterday for the new year."

"It's very nice," she said, crossing her arms where she stood.

"Get in," he said softly.

Gianna grinned. "Nope."

When she turned and headed back to her condo, he had no choice but to lock up his car and follow her. He felt himself growing harder with each step he took. She was already inside, peeling off her coat, when he reached her door.

"Gianna, I made reservations," he reminded her.

"Sounds fancy," she said. She dropped her coat and purse on the couch. "Lock up and then cancel it."

"Now who's bossy?"

Gianna grinned. "I gotta say, I understand the appeal now that I'm calling the shots. Come upstairs."

"Fucking hell. You're killing me."

Following her, he retrieved his phone from his pocket, immensely grateful for text confirmations. With one quick response, he was able to cancel the reservation without any fuss. He stepped into her room, briefly took in the soft pastel blue walls before his gaze zeroed in on the bed covered with an obscene number of pillows of various sizes. Gianna stood by the bed, waiting. He looked at her with hungry eyes.

"We'll order pizza. Maybe some wings," he said as he crossed the room to her. "I have a feeling you're going to be really hungry in an hour."

They undressed each other, tossing clothes haphazardly to the floor as they touched and caressed newly exposed flesh. Naked, they tumbled into the sea of pillows, sending half of them falling to the floor. Her body arched under his as he kissed his way from her neck to her chest, taking detours to worship each of her breasts with his tongue.

Her heart raced with something more than arousal lurking there. *What was this feeling?* She wondered. Beyond the heady pleasure that caressed her skin was a soft, tickling sensation that fluttered around her heart. It filled her, warmed her, and made her dizzy. *What was this?* She thought. And then, as his face settled between her legs, she didn't think at all.

This wasn't his plan and yet, when one of her hands grabbed the back of his head for purchase and the other landed on the wrist that held her legs open, he knew he was exactly where he needed to be. Her moans and pleas, the succulent flavor of her was all the sustenance a man could ask for.

Hunter kissed his way back up her body and pressed his lips to her neck and whispered in her ear. Then he rolled over onto his back, taking her with him. Gianna sat on his legs, curls dancing wildly around her face as she stared at him and opened the condom that he passed her to roll it on for him.

She leaned down to kiss him before rising to take him inside her. His fingers dug into her thighs as she rode him, just as she had fantasized. The slow, winding undulations of her hips were both torture and pleasure to him. He watched, enthralled, as she touched herself and worked her clit, her movements becoming increasingly wild.

He held on, knowing she was close. Held on,

knowing he was too. And then it happened. She threw back her head, moaning loudly. He watched her fall apart above him, her body glorious and glowing, and followed her over the edge.

∞∞∞∞∞∞∞∞

Later, they curled up together on her couch to watch *Psych*, bellies full of pizza and wings. Then, after a few episodes, they spent the next few hours playing Vault Hunter 2.

Occasionally, when she looked over at him, she felt that weird flutter in her stomach. But, taking her friend's advice, she tried not to think of it too much. They were having so much fun simply existing this way together. Was being in a relationship really this easy? Or was it just this way with Hunter because they had so many of the same hobbies and interests?

Whatever the reason, she enjoyed their intimate and casual activities equally.

"Are all cats this crazy at this hour? Shrek literally jumped out of the shower to attack me the moment I went in the bathroom," Hunter shared as he returned from the bathroom.

Gianna laughed. "Night time zoomies are definitely not abnormal, but I think he's just excited to have access to the bathroom at this hour. Normally at this time, all the doors would be closed up so they're not getting into shit they have no business touching."

"Huh. I had no idea." He plopped back down next to her and picked up his controller. "Maybe I should foster a cat or two to help me figure out if I can really handle being a cat dad."

"You're welcome to take my pair of assholes," she said casually. Then she paused the game as the idea settled in. "Actually. Seriously. Take my cats."

"What? You're crazy."

"No, listen. I was thinking of finding a long-term home for them until we can move into the new house. This way, I don't have to worry about locking them up when I show this place. I would also keep them there after I move in with Emilia. Living with someone else will be an adjustment for sure, but at least they won't have to constantly be in crates or getting stressed out by another house getting packed up into boxes."

"That still seems like it would be hard for them, and you. Won't you miss seeing them?"

"If they're with you, I'll see them whenever I come over," she said, slanting him a heated look.

"Oooh. Hmm," he said thoughtfully. "Well, if you trust me, I'm willing to give it a try."

Gianna's heart melted when she realized she really did trust him more than she realized. Maybe it wasn't complete, unconditional trust, but it still shocked her that they weren't that far off.

She squeezed his thigh. "I trust you."

"Then let's do it," he said, picking up her hand to place a kiss on her palm. "I see you're packing already. When are you listing this place?"

"Likely in March. It just feels easier to do a little bit at a time, you know? I'd rather not rush if the buyers want less than a thirty-day close."

"Yeah, I get that. How long have you lived here?"

She snuggled up to his side. "Since I was seventeen."

"Right. After your parents…," he recalled.

"Yes, after my DNA providers disowned me and I was emancipated."

Sensing she didn't want to talk about her parents and not really blaming her, he switched gears.

"What was your aunt like?"

"Zia Angela?" She closed her eyes as she pictured her aunt's sweet face. "A lot like me. I guess it's better to say that I'm a lot like her. She loved life. Loved to travel and meet new people. I think she would have liked you."

His own heart leapt in excitement at her confession. Maybe making her fall for him would be easier than he thought.

"I'm very likeable,"

She snorted, then yawned. "Sure, when you're not being bossy."

He chuckled. "You're tired. I should probably get going. Yeah, it's late. Are you tutoring tomorrow? Or do you have jiu-jitsu?"

Gianna glanced at the clock, so that it was nearly midnight. "You're not staying?"

"Is that really what you want?"

Gianna chuckled. "What I want? What happened to the pushy, bossy, and domineering little shit that was trying to get with me for a whole damn month?"

He angled his body so he was facing her and slid his hand up into her hair. Then, with a firm grip, he tugged her head back so he had enough space to move. He pulled her down to the couch and laid on top of her.

"And you spent a whole month pushing me away. I've switched gears because this is all new for you. I want more, and I'm not planning to settle for less. Until you're sure that you're really looking for more than a situationship, I think taking things slow is warranted."

She glared up at him. "Are you done?"

"Yeah." He released her hair and braced himself over her. "I'm done. I'll get going."

"Just a second," she said.

Before he could get up, she cupped the back of his neck with her right hand and grasped his right elbow with her other. Thinking she wanted a final kiss, Hunter leaned down to meet her halfway. But she suddenly shifted to her side and pressed her knee diagonally against his chest. Before he could ask her what she was doing, he was sent flying off the couch.

He landed on the floor with a painful thud, which was then compounded by her full weight sitting on his chest. But she didn't stay seated there. Instead, she braced her knees on either side of his body and slid up, pushing his arms over his face and locking them there with her knees.

"Well, this was a long time coming," she said cooly as she rearranged his top arm to further lock it between her thighs. "I think I've wanted to physically hurt you since I bumped into this stupidly hard chest of yours."

"Gianna," he mumbled angrily against his own arm. "What the fuck!"

"Quick lesson in jiu-jitsu. The most important. Put your knees up. Feet flat on the ground." She looked back to be sure he complied. "Yell 'tap' or stomp the ground with your foot when it hurts."

"What!?"

In response, she lifted the arm closest to his face, pressing against the other arm that rest on top of it. The movement was slight, but the discomfort was immediate.

"Ow! Tap!" He shouted and stomped his foot.

She released his arm immediately. "You're a fast

learner. The first move was called a scissor sweep. This one is a high mount arm bar."

"That's not the explanation I'm looking for," he hissed.

"Alright," she said, toying with his arm to test his limits. She stopped every time he tapped. "You know, from the very moment we met again, you haven't exactly been kind. Assuming the worst about me, jumping to conclusions when you hear something you don't like. Tonight is the third time. The final time. I won't let you keep treating me like this."

"What are you—tap! Tap!"

"You have a bad habit of fleeing every time something doesn't go your way. And every time, your opinion of me takes a hit. The first time was in high school. If only you had talked to me. Better yet, if only you'd trusted the girl who actually thought of you as a friend. The same girl who—I can't believe I'm even telling you this—had the most ridiculous little crush on you back then. Yeah, you," she added when she felt his body jolt in surprise.

"Why wouldn't I? You were my bestie's older cousin who was freakishly smart, mysteriously quiet, and awkwardly cute in this way that drew me to you. It wasn't even about looks, not really. It was the way you'd get so locked in on a problem, like the rest of the world disappeared. Or how your laugh always came a second late, like you didn't expect to find things funny but couldn't help yourself. You were different from the other guys. You never treated me like they did. You never looked at me like you were wondering when I'd put out. Even when you started tutoring me, you never made me feel stupid. I always felt like I could just be myself around you without fear of judgement or mistreatment. How could I not have had a crush on you?"

Gianna paused for a moment, checking the desire to wring his neck in frustration.

"It didn't last long, but still, it was there. And sometimes I can't help but wonder…what would've happened if either of us had done something about it?" She asked with a sigh, her face thoughtful. Then she shook her head.

"The second time was on New Years. The moment I didn't immediately fall into your arms and go along with your plans, you threw a tantrum and left. And now, tonight. Since I'm new to this, you've decided the pace of this relationship without considering what I want. You assume I'm going to treat you like I have all the other men who have briefly been in my life even though I've treated you differently from the start. You have no idea the liberties I've given you. From the manhandling, to getting in my space. I've always given you more when I would have just cut you out of my life and never looked back if you were any other man."

Annoyed, she toyed with his arm again.

"Stop! That fucking hurts!"

"Good!" She shouted suddenly. "Because you're hurting me! Give me some fucking credit for once, Hunter. It's actually pretty easy to be in relationship from my perspective. I just say yes to all the shit I normally would say fuck no to. Do you know why Fiona hissed at you? Because you're the first man she's seen in this house besides the goddamn plumber. I've never given my address to any of the guys I've slept with. How many more of my firsts do you need before you get it? Having you in my bed, hoping you'll spend the night in it…How dare you treat me like I'm not taking this seriously? How fucking dare you!"

Her breath hitched and she realized, astonishingly, that she was going to cry. Appalled, she quickly climbed off of his body to swipe angrily at the few tears that managed to escape. She took a few deep breaths, refusing to let another tear fall.

Hunter rolled over to sit on his knees just as she turned her back to him. He didn't need to see the tears. He had heard them, and the pain, so clearly in her voice. It broke his heart. He wanted her to hurt him again, to make him pay for hurting the woman he loved.

He closed his eyes, wanting to confess his feelings, but unsure if he should. He didn't think she was ready for that, but now he wondered if that was just another wrong assumption. He wasn't expecting to fall in love so quickly, and he didn't know that it came with so many minefields.

"I can't promise you that I won't hurt you again. I know that I'm going to make mistakes because I…I really want to be with you. It's a bit overwhelming. It clouds all rational thought. But I can and will admit that I was wrong, that what you're feeling is my fault, and that I need to change my behavior so that I don't hurt you again."

Gianna sighed, frustrated and annoyed. "That's a really good response, asshole."

His lips twitched. "I'm sorry? You'll have to blame the therapy."

"What else you got?" She asked and returned to the couch. She sat on the opposite side, giving him plenty of space.

"I do seem to have a bad habit of running away, of jumping to conclusions and making assumptions. I'll do my best to stop. It would help if we both try to share more of what we're feeling," he said, moving to sit on the couch as well. "Be more honest with each other or we're just going to keep hurting each other. That's another big thing you've tossed suddenly in my lap, Gianna."

She sighed. "Fine. I should have told you. I'm sorry."

"Don't be. I'm sorry. I set myself up buying that car because of you and assuming you weren't as bought in as I was as a result."

"Bought a car? For me? You're joking."

"Nope. I've wanted to get a second car for over a year. I finally did it because I have a girlfriend."

"Oh." Her heart tripped. "A girlfriend?"

"Yes," he said quietly, moving closer. "You're changing so much to let me be with you and I bought a car for the sole purpose of whisking you away. I want you to be mine. What do you want, Gianna?"

"You," she said with a sigh as he pulled her into his arms. "Just you."

"Then I'm yours."

CHAPTER 12

Gianna slept fitfully, unable to settle into a deep slumber despite the soothing warmth of Hunter's body nestled beside her. Surrounded by the comforts of her own home, she expected to sleep as soundly as she had their first time together.

But while she had experienced sleeping in another man's bed, even if it was infrequent, she was keenly aware that Hunter was the first man she had ever lain with in this space.

She rolled over to face him, careful not to disturb the stillness between them. In the soft hush of the room, lit only by the faintest glow slipping in through the curtains, she waited for her eyes to adjust. She could just make out the shape of his lips. Soft, parted slightly with sleep. And the rise and fall of his chest beneath the thin sheet tangled at his waist. His breathing was steady and quiet, but each exhale fanned gently across her face, warm and rhythmic, grounding her more than she expected.

Lying this close, listening to the subtle sounds of him made everything outside the room feel impossibly far away. Having him here, sharing this kind of stillness in the dark, felt...significant.

The last few days hadn't exactly gone smoothly. She unloaded on him, exposing deeply flawed and damaged parts of her personality that most sane people would keep hidden. Instead of running away, he stepped in, accepting her exactly as she was while subtly hinting that she could be more. Not better. Just more.

Just as she had when he had tutored in high school, she wanted, desperately, to prove him right.

Having him here didn't just feel significant, it felt right. He had captured her body, her heart. Now, she wanted to prove that he made the right choice.

She gently brushed a finger over his chin, her thoughts spinning, searching for a way to show him. When she finally had an idea, she sat up, glanced at the clock on her dresser, and cringed. It was nearly six. She hated waking up early on weekends, but it was pointless to continue to pretend to sleep.

Quietly as she could, she eased from the bed, then, phone in hand, she crawled around on all fours to gather his clothes. Slipping into her ensuite, she noted the size of his clothes before throwing on her own sweats and sweatshirt.

Thankfully, he was still asleep when she left the bedroom and she hoped he would stay that way until she returned. Once inside her car, she drove to the only department store that was open at this godforsaken hour.

Hunter hadn't planned to stay the night so he didn't have any clothes or toiletries. Since she rarely had guests, the most she could give him was a towel. She couldn't even offer him a toothbrush because she used an electric one.

Wanting him to be comfortable, and stay a while longer, she quickly made her way through the store, picking up deodorant, a toothbrush, black sweatpants, and the brand of boxers he had worn that day. She meant to be quick in the graphic tee section, but she ended up spending more time perusing their options to find one that she felt suited his personality. With a shirt that read, "I paused my game to be here" in hand, she headed to the register to checkout.

Glancing at the clock, she drove to BJ Cinnamon, a family-owned bakery in Folsom, for a dozen donuts and a few breakfast croissant sandwiches. It was just after seven now, and while it was possible that he was still sleeping, she wouldn't be surprised if he was up and wondering where she went.

When she let herself back in her condo, soft sunlight filtered through the house from the opened curtains. The scent of coffee, freshly brewed, filled the air, letting her know that he had made himself at home and found the coffee pods. As she placed the food on the counter, she heard the telltale sounds of lapping.

Peering around the counter, she saw Shrek and Fiona happily devouring wet cat food, something she usually only gave them at the end of the day. For some reason, this made her grin as her heart all but overflowed with joy. He really did settle in if he went as far to find the cat food, and she couldn't be more pleased.

Since he wasn't present, she ventured upstairs and found him in her room. He had opened the curtains here as well, and light spilled in to caress his brown skin as he stood next to her bed. Wearing only boxers, Hunter appeared to be finishing making her bed and tossed pillows on it with a scowl on his face. She felt her blood hum with need, unsure if she appreciated looking at his body or that he would do that for her. Resisting the urge to undo his work by shoving him on that bed, she leaned against the door frame instead.

"Good morning. Has my bed offended you?"

"Not the bed. The pillows," he sneered, tossing another haphazardly on top. "Why do you have so many? And why don't you have something to put them in when they're not suffocating your bed?"

"Well now I kind of want to get more, just to torture you," she said with a cheeky grin. She crossed the room to him. "Let me do that. Here, take this."

"What is this?" he asked after accepting the bag. Then he blinked in surprise when he saw what was inside. "You bought all this for me?"

"Yeah. I figured you didn't have a fresh pair of clothes since you didn't plan to stay here last night. Now you have stuff you can leave here for next time."

Hunter stared in silence as she casually reorganized the pillows as if what she had done wasn't a big deal. Maybe to her, it wasn't. Or maybe she didn't realize that for some couples, making space for your significant other's personal items in your own home was a pretty momentous step in a relationship.

Since he couldn't decide if it would be better to tell her or not, he simply carried the bag into the ensuite bathroom to change and brush his teeth. It might be easier just to keep it to himself so he didn't make her feel uncomfortable or embarrassed. She was likely just being thoughtful, and he really appreciated it. By the time he was done, she joined him to brush her own teeth.

Hunter grinned at her through the mirror. "Thanks for all this."

She mumbled something, the sound completely muffled under the whirl of her electric toothbrush. Unable to help himself, he toyed with her hair while he waited.

"Thanks for making the bed. And for feeding the cats."

"Fiona was still a bit cautious around me so I figured it was the easiest way to soften her up."

"Figured as much. Do you want any more coffee? I picked up donuts and breakfast sandos as well."

Hunter felt a slow grin creep across his face as he watched her. "You really went all out for me this morning."

"You needed food and clothing," she dismissed with a shrug. "Plus, I figured it would keep you here a while longer before you had to go."

"Go? Gianna," he said darkly. "I'm not going anywhere until I reward you for taking care of me this way. Do you have plans today? You never answered me last night."

"No. With it being new year week—"

Hunter cut her off by grabbing her sweatshirt and tugging her to him. His hand dove in her hair to hold the back of her head. He nibbled on her lips as he spoke.

"Good. Then here's what we're going to do today. First, I'm going to fuck you. Maybe right here in the bathroom. I haven't decided."

He turned her suddenly, trapping her between the counter and his body. Feeling him pressed against her, already hard, her breath hitched in response. Her eyes lifted to meet his in the mirror and in them was part fear, part desire.

"Not here then," he said gently, understanding that look now. He turned her back to face him again. "Or not that position?"

"Not…that position," she said, avoiding eye contact.

"That's alright." He wrapped his arms around her waist to lift her. "It's alright."

Gianna cupped the back of his head while he carried her inside the bedroom to lay her on the bed. He settled his body on top of hers.

"Thank you," she whispered, a little embarrassed, though she knew it was foolish to feel that way. "What's the rest of the plan for today?"

"Breakfast. Sex. Laundry. Sex." He lifted her right leg so he could press into her heat. "Then I'll take you on a proper date for dinner."

"With sex to follow, I'm guessing."

He chuckled. "I was going to say dessert but sex works too."

∞∞∞∞∞∞∞

He blinked and found himself in March.

Hunter's weekdays were spent on the Jonhson-Maffucci job site. On an occasional weeknight and damn near every weekend, he was with Gianna. Sometimes they went out for lunch or dinner, sometimes they spent the day at one of their places.

Each time he saw her, he tried to do something to get under her skin. He randomly bought her flowers, her favorite sweet treat or food, and even treated her to a manicure and pedicure one weekend when she was feeling particularly stressed out about a project at work.

He stayed up late on more nights than he cared to admit building her a wooden storage trunk out of one by six boards to hold her obscene pillow collection every night. Her face when he delivered it last weekend had been priceless and made up for loss of sleep.

He was content with where their relationship was going. The only time he felt any unease, unfortunately, was when she became the topic of his crew's conversations.

"What about the job we did in South Sac two years ago. The guy's daughter kept coming around to check shit out because she knew she'd get the house when he croaked. Big ass boobs but no ass."

Hunter looked askance at Todd. "No. How the hell do you even remember that?"

"I keep telling you this guy is a stalker," Eddie said. "In the last two months, he's named damn near every female client or acquaintance we've had since he started working at Hall Construction."

Jose chuckled as he put on his tool belt. "Can you blame the guy? He's got no game at the bar or club, so naturally he's desperate to try to pull one of our clients."

"Fuck you," Todd fired back. "I'm only asking because I thought we had a rule against dating clients."

"Right, right. Because you got no game. And we all know that you don't give a shit about rules with the long list you've provided," Jose sneered. "You've definitely gone back and hit on some of these women."

"There's a rule against sexually harassing any client, both past and present," Hunter reminded them with a pointed look.

Given Todd's troubled history, and his disturbing recall of past female clients, Eddie's accusation hit a little too close to home. He sincerely hoped that Todd hadn't been causing problems by harassing or stalking former clients.

"It's not like that. I just have a good memory for good looking women," Todd explained.

"I still say Hunter's making it up," Eddie said. "Why else keep it a secret?"

"How about because it's none of your damn

business?" Hunter said, annoyed.

"Damn, it's like that?" Eddie questioned. "We've been working together for so fucking long and we can't even get the name of the girl you've been fucking for two months?"

Hunter sighed, feeling a bit guilty. "I'm sorry. We both want to keep things on the DL for now. It's complicated. When it's not, I'll let you know."

Eddie eyed him suspiciously. "You got me thinking it's a current client. Like the one coming today."

"She's not," he said calmly, forcing himself not to panic. "You do know that Sam is married. To a woman."

"Just admit you're banging a former client's wife already, Hunter," Jose teased. "We don't judge you!"

"Nah, I'm calling bullshit!" Eddie insisted.

"You didn't see that hickey he had last week before he covered it up," Pablo said, finally joining the conversation. "Besides, I know the signs of a morning quickie that ends up making you late for work."

"Oooh a sneaky link, huh?" Jose guessed.

Eddie chuckled. "That Netflix and chill!"

"Can you guys get to work already?" Hunter demanded, embarrassed and annoyed because they had landed effortlessly on the truth.

Jose and Eddie followed him to the backyard from the basement, but they didn't stop teasing him. He couldn't blame them. This whole thing was his own damn fault. He had been so caught up in pursuing Gianna that he refused to consider the implications of dating a client. They really didn't have any clearly spelled out rules against it, but it wasn't something he wanted to encourage so he and Gianna agreed to tell them that his girlfriend was a former client instead. He just knew that he was going to be in for some shit when the truth finally came out.

He pushed that problem to the back of his mind and focused on what needed to happen today. After the thirty-day close, they waited an additional month for district approvals and county permits. During that time, they could only do light demo and site preparation. Once the permits were in, James and Naomi joined them on the site to lay plumbing while they built the formwork for the slab addition.

Hunter caught movement out of the corner of his eye. On the other side of the yard, Gianna, Emilia, and Sam waited in front of the garage, each holding a pink box that could only hold donuts. They were here to watch the cement mixer pour the slab.

"Clients are here," Hunter called out and went to greet them.

Eddie grabbed Jose's arm to hold him back before he could follow Hunter.

"Yo, doesn't that woman look familiar? The one with the long brunette hair."

"Yeah, a bit," Jose replied after following his gaze.

The woman in question had a gorgeous smile and wore a sharp black pantsuit with a red floral blouse. The color jogged his memory. Jose's eyes nearly popped out in shock when it hit him.

"Oh, shit! Is that…I think that's the brunette Todd was bitching about!"

Eddie started laughing. "That guy has the worst fucking luck. Always wanting women that he can't possibly have."

Jose snorted. "You think this will stop him? Between her showing up again and Hunter dating a former client, he'll do anything to get at her."

"Bet," Eddie agreed. "Twenty says he blows it."

"Fuck that. That's a sucker's bet. Aye, Todd! Get out here."

"What?" Todd grumbled, walking out of the basement to drop two by fours at their feet.

"Your dream girl is over there flirting with Hunter," Eddie teased.

Todd looked over. He recognized her immediately, and his gut burned with anger. He never forgot the ones who made him look like a fool. Watching her smile so freely at a man who had been born with little more than a hammer in his hand only angered him further. Women had such shitty taste.

The crew went over to join Hunter. Todd elbowed his way through them to stand in front of Gianna.

"Thank you," he said, smiling at her before peaking in the box. "All glazed. My favorite."

"They only brought glazed, dumbass," Jose mumbled under his breath, trying not to laugh.

"No problem," Gianna said, grinning in amusement.

"Most of you have met Sam," Hunter said loudly, eager to cover up his employee's behavior. "This is her wife Emilia, and her sister-in-law, Gianna. Pablo, Jose, Eddie, and Todd will be here consistently throughout the project."

"Such a small crew," Sam said, clearly concerned.

"Just for today. I'll be pulling some apprentices from Hall's Helpers for other projects. Plus, you know James and Naomi have their own team as well," he added, reminding them of his twin brother and sister.

They all looked over when they heard a loud beeping sound.

"That'll be the cement mixer," Hunter said. "You

guys have some time to wolf down a few donuts while it gets in place. Eddie, can you take our clients over to get hardhats?"

"I got it!" Todd interjected. "Follow me, Gianna."

Hunter couldn't help but grind his teeth together as Todd led them away.

"If they're going to be a distraction, I'll make them leave."

"There's that sweet demeanor that landed you a girlfriend," Pablo said, rolling his eyes. "Don't worry, jefe. We'll keep Todd in check."

Hunter sighed as he went to meet the truck driver. Somehow, he just knew this whole thing with keeping Gianna a secret would blow up in his face.

As the months went by, they did, in fact, eagerly and sometimes cruelly keep Todd in check. Hunter learned that Gianna had rejected Todd's advances at a chance meeting last year and the crew was all too happy to remind Todd of his failure.

Todd made his situation worse, however, by continuing to assert that he still had a chance. Gianna came by once or twice a month, and although she never gave him any reason to think she was interested in him, Todd believed otherwise. His coworkers teased and taunted him for days after she came by.

At times, Hunter wondered if he should step in to protect his friend, but he also thought some of it was well deserved. Now that he wasn't the center of their attention, he could sit back and watch things playout with a new perspective he hadn't had before.

Gianna, always friendly and approachable, treated everyone the same. It made him see things exactly as she had said. Some men really did purposefully misconstrue women's every action. Her kindness was seen as interest, her smile as an invitation. He shuddered to think of what Todd thought about her pants suits and dresses.

And so, as Todd's boss, he felt slightly guilty that his crew kept bringing Todd back to reality, especially when they were too harsh. But, as Gianna's boyfriend, he didn't give not one flying fuck.

CHAPTER 13

"You're nothing but the hired help building her dream home. She's practically oozing wealth and privilege and yet you think she's going to settle for your pathetic ass? What a joke!"

For some reason, Hunter stopped short when he heard this, those words waking up a part of him that he thought were buried. As the feelings rose to the surface, he remained frozen in the hallway while Jose continued to insult Todd yet again.

"What did you fucking say?" Todd demanded.

"You heard me," Jose jeered. "She's not having this place built to invite you to live in it. When this project this over, she'll move in and forget you ever existed."

Hunter heard a sudden shuffling movement, raised

voices, and a stream of curse words that finally snapped him out of it. He dashed into the room to find Pablo holding Todd back while Jose sneered derisively down his nose at him.

"That's enough!" Hunter hollered, drawing their attention. "It's been six fucking months of this bullshit. Both of you need to let this go. If I hear either one of you talk about Gianna again, I'm kicking you off this job. Todd, walk it off and then go work on the basement with Eddie. Jose, stop running your mouth and get back to work."

Hunter watched Todd slither off, his face pinched with anger. Feeling a headache starting to creep up, he went down to the garage for water. Trying to calm down, he dragged over his clipboard from the folding table they set up to hold the plans for the home. He tried focusing on it, but for some reason he kept recalling what Jose as said.

Refusing to let those thoughts out, he tossed the clipboard on the table and went out to find something to do. For the next three hours he pushed himself, enduring the increasing heat to haul lumber, carry tile, transport drywall, or lift bags of cement.

By the time the workday came to an end, he was utterly exhausted. Sitting in traffic on the drive home only exacerbated his headache, making him regret not staying on site to finish odds and ends until traffic died down.

But she would be there, he reminded himself. The source of his joy. His pleasure.

His pain.

That slimy trendle of doubt burst through the cracks once more. Refusing to let it show, he shoved it back down and buried it once more.

Sure enough, Gianna's car was parked in his driveway when he pulled up to his house. After some back and forth, he finally convinced her that it made sense for her to have a key to his place so she could check on Shrek and Fiona after they moved in two weeks ago. She seemed to understand that this was a big step in their relationship, one that her reluctance told him that she wasn't prepared to take.

In the end, his logic was undeniable so she had taken his key.

Hunter climbed from the car, his body weary, and let himself inside in his house. It was Friday and now that her cats lived with him, he expected that she would stay the entire weekend. Spending the weekend together, whether at her place or his, had become their unspoken routine.

Sure enough, he glanced down by his door and saw her overnight bag. Immediately, his mood soured further. It wasn't the first time he had that reaction and he couldn't quite figure out why it happened every time he saw that bag.

Kicking off his shoes, Hunter looked across the room and found Gianna in his kitchen. In tight, red bike shorts and a loose white tank, she stood out against his dark gray cabinetry and butcher block countertops. As was becoming usual, her presence in his space felt like a light breaking through all the dark that he hadn't even been aware was there.

Though he still felt some of the weight of the day, it was easy to push it to the back of his mind when she looked up to smile at him.

"Hi. I just finished prepping everything for the sandwiches," she said, crossing the room to peck him on the lips. "You look beat though. Sit for a bit."

He resisted the urge to pull her close so he could kiss her longer. "Later. I need a shower first."

Hunter emptied his pockets on to the table before walking to his ensuite bathroom. He turned the water on before stripping, and, without waiting for the water to heat, he climbed inside.

The cold water shocked his system, chasing away those doubts temporarily. He stood under the spray, water splashing over his head and wished he could wash them away completely.

"Your phone is going off like crazy."

Hunter looked up to see Gianna place his phone on the counter, her eyes roaming over him. Her heated look let him know exactly where her thoughts were headed, and his own followed that same path in response.

"Come here."

She shook her head in refusal, though her eyes continued to devour him.

"You looked so tired when you came in," she reminded him.

"That look woke me up. See?" He turned so she could see the effect she was having on his body. "Get in."

Unable to resist, Gianna slipped out of her shirt and shorts. His shower was square shaped and it was just big enough for two. Pressed together after she stepped inside, their bodies slid intimately against each other as water sloshed over them. Lips locked, they kissed lazily as their hands explored heated skin.

Gianna captured him in her hands, her fist tight, and slowly stroked him.

Hunter chuckled breathlessly. "Went right in for the kill, huh?"

"What can I say? I'm hungry." Then she dropped to her knees. "Very hungry."

Hunter fell back against the shower wall when she sucked the head of his cock into her mouth. Her hand continued its deliberate caress as her tongue teased him. He let out a string of intelligible praise comingled with low, guttural moans. The wet heat of her mouth combined with the wet heat of the water had his senses in overload. Unbearably aroused, his hips started thrusting of their own accord. He pictured himself fucking that beautiful mouth until he poured every drop of cum down her throat. Feeling an orgasm nipping at him and worried he would lose control and do just that, he placed his hand on hers.

"Gianna," he gasped, forcing out the command. "Fuck. Stop."

She stopped sucking him, but her hand never stopped moving. She looked up at him as she licked her lips.

"No. We don't have a—"

He cupped her chin, stopping those words as he pulled her up. Once she was standing, he swooped in to capture her lips and press her against the wall. Grabbing one thigh, he lifted her leg until he could get his arm under and then repeated it with her other leg. Once he had her balanced against the wall and on his arms, he thrust inside of her.

"Condom," Gianna moaned.

"Too late. I can't stop," he growled, thrusting deeper and harder. "I'm sorry."

"Liar," she rasped, moving her hand between them to touch herself.

"I swear," he said between a sound that was half moan, half laugh. "Ah, fuck, you feel so good. Don't be mad. I'm sorry."

"Shut up and fuck me, Hunter."

He shuddered in pleasure and shut up to fuck her until he spilled every drop of cum inside her.

Hunter released her, needing his own arms to balance himself on shaky legs. She leaned heavily against the shower wall and stared at him, a self-satisfied and sleepy haze in her eyes. He was too worried about the line he crossed to recognize the look.

"Shit, I… I'm sorry. I shouldn't have—"

"Why are you apologizing? We've been seeing each other exclusively for months. I assumed this would happen eventually. It's not a problem for me. Unless it's a problem for you."

"It's not. I just should have asked before," he insisted.

She pressed a finger to his lips to silence him. "My dear, sweet, always in control Hunter completely lost control. Over me. Sir, you're interrupting me as I bask in the magnificent glory of this truly monumental accomplishment."

I fucking love you, he thought. He wanted to say the words, but he chuckled awkwardly instead before swallowing him back. He didn't know why, but he couldn't say them yet.

When they were clean and dressed, Hunter checked his phone, which had continued to ping incessantly the entire time they were in the shower. He knew it was his family from the sheer number of times his phone beeped.

They were making plans for Father's Day. Hunter stared down at his phone with a frown on his face. It wasn't that there was anything wrong with the holiday. He just suddenly realized that he wanted Gianna to go with him. Wanted to introduce his family to the woman he loved.

Jose's words resurfaced, and dug right in to uncover that pocket of doubt that he had only just shoved down again. He didn't know why he was like this. Why he let anxiety eat away at him this way. It was foolish to think that it was too soon, especially after tonight. So why did he find himself hesitant to ask her?

Why couldn't he tell her that he was in love with her?

He went in the kitchen, wondering why he felt this way. Gianna was washing something in the sink, likely waiting on him. Her sandwich was already put together and waiting on the dining room table. He set his phone down and started building his own sandwich.

"Who was texting you? I don't think I've ever heard you phone go off that much at one time."

"It's my family. They're trying to put a plan together for Father's Day next weekend."

"That sounds fun," she hummed before drying her hands. She went to the table and sat, picking up food. "So, I won't see you next weekend then. Pity, but that works out. Emilia has been wanting me to go furniture shopping with her."

Inside the kitchen, Hunter flinched, and all those content feelings he had after being with her in the shower fell away into that pocket of doubt as it widened. He teetered on the edge, wobbling as he tried not to fall in too. Oblivious, Gianna continued chatting, going on about furniture and décor for Emilia and Sam's place. Dejectedly, he fixed his sandwich, barely hearing a word.

It wasn't a big deal, he told himself. She just wasn't there yet. It was fine. Not everyone fell in love quickly.

Just because he fell first didn't mean that she wouldn't be far behind. She was here, with him, and that was all that mattered.

It was only a matter of time before he captured her heart.

∞∞∞∞∞∞

Despite his reassurances, Hunter continued to be haunted by his own doubts. Instead of talking to her about his fears, he threw himself into work, implanting himself in nearly every project, no matter how big or small. His efforts paid off by putting the project slightly ahead of schedule.

Unfortunately, this only seemed to exacerbate his mood.

On a hot and quiet Saturday afternoon in late June, Hunter walked through the construction site, taking notes on their progress. He ran a smaller crew for a half day on Saturdays, keeping the choice to work an option for his team. In this way, those who needed or wanted a break or extra money could take it, and they could stay on schedule with the renovations.

Judging from his list, he expected to be able to turn the keys over to the homeowners in about a month, barring major problems or other delays. Much of what they needed was either already on site or on its way. He could see the finished project so clearly in his head now.

Gianna was also closing out an important step in this journey today. Her aunt's condo had been sold and with the closing date set for Tuesday, she was spending this weekend moving out.

He should have felt excitement, even relief to see this project come to an end. They managed to keep everything on budget and on time. There hadn't been any complications or delays with materials. No injuries on the job. That such a large project had been so successful brought him a lot a pride in his work

And yet, each day, he felt fear and anxiety crawling under his skin. He couldn't name exactly why. Or maybe, he could and just didn't want to.

"Hunter!" Eddie shouted, jolting him from his thoughts after calling him three times.

"Yeah, what?" Hunter said, turning to face him and trying to be calm.

Eddie snorted. "We've been calling you on the walkie for five minutes, but you didn't hear a damn word I said, did you?"

"No, sorry," he snapped. "What do you want?"

"I was just telling you that we're going to head out. Don't snap at me just because you've fucked up with Gianna!"

He stared for a full thirty seconds before he could think of a response, and even then, he only managed to say, "What?"

Eddie sighed. "Look, I wasn't going to say anything about you two, but you've been distracted and moody since Father's Day and it's fucking annoying. What's going on with you two?"

"I'm not…we're not…" he trailed off.

"Save it," Eddie said, rolling his eyes. "I told you I didn't buy that bullshit about you dating a former client. It had to be someone current. My choices were Gianna or Mrs. Buckhead."

Hunter gaped at him. "Mrs. Buckhead is a sixty-year-old married woman."

"I'm not one to judge."

"The fuck you aren't," Hunter snapped. "How did you figure it out? Does anyone else know?"

"Because I know you. You're usually casual and friendly with clients, but with Gianna, it's always very distant, very professional. Like you're both trying really hard to look that way."

"I don't see how—"

"Hey, guys," Trevor interrupted as he joined them in the basement unit. "Can I leave or is there a problem?"

"Hey, Trevor. Why did you figure out that Hunter was banging Gianna?"

"Eddie!"

The young apprentice stalled for a minute, still getting used to the abrasive banter of the older crew he joined on this job. Embarrassed, he scratched the back of his head.

"Um, your brother James mentioned that you all went to high school together. When the guys said you had a girlfriend who was also a client, I just assumed…"

"Fuuuuck," Hunter cursed up at the ceiling. "Everybody knows."

"Everybody except Todd has put it together, but he's purposefully living in a state of denial where he actually has a chance with Gianna. You should probably put his pathetic ass out of his misery."

Hunter rubbed his face. "Fucking hell. Why didn't you guys say anything?"

Eddie shrugged. "It's not a rule, but seeing it play out, it should be. You're renovating this house for her, and for all you know, you'll never see the inside of it again after you hand her the keys. I'm not saying she's using you!" He added when Hunter turned on him, his face pinched with anger. "Just that you don't know how the future will play out. Her future is here, but who knows where yours is? No wonder your mood has been so shitty. None of us want to be in your shoes, so we didn't say anything. It might not be a written rule, but you can bet none of us will try it after seeing the two of you."

"Great. Fucking great. Thanks. You guys can go. I'll lock up."

He made one final circuit of the site, making sure all of the windows and doors were locked before he left. He finally understood the painful discomfort that lurked in that pocket he had tried to bury. He understood why this entire situation bothered him so much. He drove home, trying to patch up the pieces inside him that had begun to splinter.

In the six months he and Gianna had dated, she had shared so much about her hopes and ideas for the future. From the tutors she planned to hire now that she had a brick-and-mortar space, to the STEM scholarship that was nearly ready to be launched. Or how she would decorate her new living room for the holidays and the family dinners they would have. She had so many plans.

Even today, when she was at her condo with the movers. She didn't ask him to help and had even turned down his offer to help. He knew she had hired movers, but he still felt that as her boyfriend, he should have been there to support her and the entire process.

Feeling stupid, Hunter let himself inside his home. Shrek and Fiona strode over to greet him. So much of their stuff was now strewn throughout his house. Cat trees, scratching pads, and cat toys. But nothing else that belonged to Gianna was here. Her cats lived here. She stayed over most weekends because of that. And still, she never left so much as a toothbrush or hair tie in the bathroom.

The small overnight bag she carried in each time she arrived was like a suitcase full of distance. It was the unspoken space between them, and it broke his heart a little bit every time. He couldn't shake the feeling that she had one foot out the door. It was his own damn fault for wanting more so quickly. For falling in love with her almost as soon as they got started.

He wanted to say something. To ask why she still packed up like a guest in a home that had become half hers. But he didn't. Because if he asked, he might hear the answer he feared most.

∞∞∞∞∞∞∞

"This is weird," Valerie said quietly. "I can't imagine how it feels for you."

"Definitely weird," Gianna agreed, looking around the living room. She was finally saying goodbye to the condo that had been her safe place for half of her life.

"This place hasn't been empty since Zia first moved in. Even when Emilia moved in and out, even when I moved in, there was always something here. I can't believe we'll never be back here again."

London hugged her and did her best impression of Baymax. "Zia is here."

Gianna let out a watery laugh. "You're such a nerd."

"Okay, kettle," she said with a grin.

"When will your family be here?" Valerie asked. "I don't want you to be alone."

Gianna smiled. "Soon. It's okay, really. We've known since Zia passed away that this day would come. Emilia and I have been talking about it since we put an offer on the house too."

Valerie shook her head. "I still can't believe she wrote into her will that you must sell this place within ten years of her passing in order to have her assets paid out."

"She knows us too well," Gianna admitted with a shrug. "We would have held on to this place just to hold on to her, and she didn't want that. She wanted us to use it to do something as big as what we're doing now. I know she would have been so happy with what we're doing, so it's hard to feel really sad."

"That's good," London said. "Why didn't bring Shrek and Fiona back for the night?"

Gianna shook her head. "They're doing so good with Hunter. I don't want to mess them up until it's time to move them in to the new house."

Valerie grinned. "I simply cannot picture Hunter with cats."

"They're fucking adorable," Gianna laughed. "Sometimes I swear they prefer him! It's so rude!"

"They're not the only one who prefers him! We don't hang out as much anymore," London whined.

"We're all busy," Gianna insisted. "You and Tony are always together, and don't even get me started on the married couple!"

"What can I say?" Valerie grinned. "I like sleeping with my husband."

"There was a time when I would have been so mad at you for bragging, but now that I'm getting banged on a regular, I can't complain."

London laughed. "So, things are good with you and Hunter?"

"Obviously," she teased. "Name one guy I've been with this long."

"Girl," London said, holding up one finger. "Hunter is the *only* guy I can name. I don't know about any other!"

"Honestly, you never will, and that's mostly because I've completely forgotten about them," Gianna laughed.

"You're a mess," London said with a laugh.

"Has he gone to a family dinner?" Valerie inquired.

"Hmm? No. Why would he?"

London stared at her. "Because he's your boyfriend?"

Gianna blinked. "And?"

"Huh. I just had a flashback to Valerie's wedding, except now I fully realize exactly how annoying I was."

"What does that mean?" Gianna said with a frown.

She recalled what Gianna had said to her. "Can you be less of a dick? Why are you treating him that way?"

"What?" Gianna gaped at her. "What are you talking about? Treating who what way?"

"Hunter!" London shook her head. "I'm going to start calling you Shrek and him Fiona."

"You still have a wall up and Donkey wants to kick it down. She's not ready so we'll leave her be, London."

Gianna's heart pounded loudly in her chest, like there was something trying to force its way out behind the wall that she was suddenly painfully aware was there.

"Ready for what?" she asked.

Valerie only shook her head, unwilling to say more.

"You're freaking me out. I'm actually a little worried about him. About us. If there's something you know…"

Valerie leaned over the counter. "Girl, start with that next time. What's up?"

"I'm probably just reading into this. He's been working really hard on our house. Most nights, he's too tired to do anything. I keep telling myself it's just because he's exhausted, but it just feels like he's being a little distant. For some reason, I feel like he's pulling away. But I don't know why he would."

"Is that why he didn't help you move today?" London asked.

"No. I told him to stay home. Naomi said he's been jumping on every little project. I just wanted him to take a break. But maybe it's something else. Maybe it's whatever you're talking about. I thought about asking him but I still feel like I might be making something out of nothing so I haven't said anything yet."

"Are you sure you want us to speculate?" Valerie asked.

Gianna closed her eyes and spoke truthfully. "I'm in love with him. Pretty sure I've been careening down that path since day one. If there is something I'm doing wrong… I need to hear it. Whether I'm ready or not."

London gently rubbed her shoulder. "You've always been friendly, always been kind and welcoming. But when it comes to letting people in your most intimate circles… You have a wall there, Shrek. I'm sure Hunter sees it to. You may have let Hunter get close in other ways, but you're still holding back. You're still keeping him at an emotional distance so it'll be easier for you to walk away if it comes to that."

Gianna went silent. She couldn't respond because

there was too much truth to what London was saying.

"Hunter is all about family," Valerie said quietly. "His entire family. And sharing everyone in it. What have you shared when it comes to family?"

"Of course I've shared them! I can't count how many lunches and dinners we had together while we were house hunting."

London sent her a pointed look. "And after you were done house hunting?"

"You said you never invited him to your monthly dinner with Emilia," Valerie reminded her gently.

"I never even considered it," she said sadly. "I can see that it probably made him think that I didn't want him to get close to my family."

"Maybe try taking a few of those bricks out of the wall and see if that closes the distance. Invite him to the next family dinner," London said, giving her a comforting squeeze. "If things don't get better after that, then I say you two need to have a conversation."

Gianna nodded her head quietly.

"You said he's being working a lot," Valerie said, wanting to change the subject. "How are the renovations coming along? When will you move in?"

"I feel weird saying 'thankfully', but, thankfully, it was a relatively dry winter and spring," she said, grateful to move on. "We are definitely going to have another drought this year, but at least the house will get done sooner."

"Yay?" London questioned.

"Ugh. Exactly. Hunter thinks they may be able to get the basement unit ready after the Fourth. Once they give us the go ahead, Emilia and I are going to move some furniture in. It will probably be too loud to work there during the day, but it will be nice to have that space set up before we move in. It will take forever to unpack."

"Will it be done in August as planned?" London asked.

"Hunter is pretty confident that we'll be in for our family dinner on that first Wednesday in August. I'll be sure to invite him this time."

Valerie's phone starting ringing. She glanced down at it with a sigh.

"That's Jun. I'm going to be late if we don't get going. I still have to drop off this carless freeloader."

"Okay. Thanks for your help today. With everything."

"We wanted to say goodbye to Zia, too," London shared.

"And we want you and Hunter to be happy."

Gianna smiled. "Thanks."

They left just as Emilia arrived with her family. Soon the empty home was filled with their voices and noise as they talked and set up air mattresses in the living room.

It was the first Wednesday of the month, and it was a special day, one that she cherished above many things. Gianna was ready to relax and recharge. She wanted to let go of the outside world and all its troubles until tomorrow.

She sat with her family on the floor around a box where a photo of Zia sat. They chatted about their day, their week, their month as they ate pizza. She tried to follow along with the conversation, to engage and participate.

But her head and her heart was somewhere else. She couldn't fully immerse herself in the last night in this house and say her final goodbye to the life Zia had given her by taking her in.

Gianna looked at her sister. She gazed at Sam and Ciara. She loved them so much. She counted herself lucky to have such amazing people in her life. But someone was missing from this gathering. It was usually Zia's presence that she wished for.

Tonight, however, she knew that it was Hunter who was missing.

CHAPTER 14

Gianna couldn't find time to talk to Hunter. Determined to deliver on his promise to have the basement office finished by the 4th of July, Hunter was unavailable most nights and weekends. She saw him briefly last Tuesday, but the dogged tired look in his eyes prevented her from dragging him into a deep conversation. After her conversation with London and Valerie, she worried that it was more than exhaustion that kept him away.

Despite her nerves, she walked up to her new home on a ridiculously hot Monday morning to see the finished basement.

Hunter was hovering just outside the basement door, leaning against the frame with one shoulder, likely trying to stay cool in the heavy summer air while he waited for her. Still, he looked calm and collected.

Her heart tripped at the sight of him. There was something about the way he filled the space, solid and grounded, like he belonged there. Like he belonged in the home that he had built for her and her sister.

His goatee was overdue for a trim, the edges a little uneven, but the roughness worked in his favor. Her hands itched to touch, missing the feel of him, even though it had barely been a week since they last touched.

"Hey, Hunter!"

"Welcome home," he said quietly as he pushed against the doorway to stand.

Hearing him say those words made her heart sigh. She wanted to switch places with him and welcome him home too.

Instead, she grinned and tried to feign excitement. "I'm ready!"

She didn't have to fake it once she was inside. Hunter watched as Gianna spun in a circle inside the living room, her face alive with joy. She squealed as she made her way to the L-shaped kitchen to run her hands lovingly over the small island. The cabinets were the same sage colored walls in Emilia's house to pay homage to where they'd come from. The countertops were a sparkling white quartz. Though it was a basement walkout, the space didn't lack for light. As the light hit her, it made her excitement shine even brighter.

"Hunter this is just…incredible. It's bigger than I thought. Brighter too. These windows!" She dashed back into the living room space and pointed up at the window near the ceiling. "What is this one?"

"Horizontal picture window," he explained. "Even though the house next door will block direct sunlight, having it still allows some natural light in."

"It's amazing! The front door being all glass lets in a lot of light too. I want to see the bathroom!"

She squealed and ran to the bathroom, then squealed even louder when she saw that the walls had been painted.

"You painted for us!"

Hunter grinned, following after her to take in the sage walls. They had done a simple four-piece bathroom, with the shower and tub combined. The vanity was white on white to help brighten the space.

"Just in here. Trust me. It's a pain to paint in the bathroom once everything is in. And speaking of paint, you still haven't chosen any colors for your house."

Gianna glanced at him over her shoulder as she moved to the bedroom next.

"White is fine. We—I mean, that decision can be made later. After."

"After you move in?" He questioned, confused. "Trust me, it's best if you do it now."

"Later," she insisted and turned her attention to the bedroom.

Again, they had gone for simple, but used mirrored barn doors for the closet instead of regular doors to add some style and flair to the room.

Gianna sighed happily and all but floated to him. "Hunter…I know we agreed no PDA here, but I really, really must kiss you."

His lips quirked in amusement. "Is that right?"

She pushed him into the hallway so they would at least be away from the window. Wrapping her arms around his waist, she tilted her head up to pour herself into the kiss. All the delight and anticipation, her appreciation for all the hours of work he put into this. She felt so much for him in this moment that she could hardly name them, though love was certainly at the forefront.

It had only been a few weeks since he last had her, but in that time, his doubts and concerns only grew. And so, he kissed her with a desperation that he couldn't contain. He wanted to take her, right here in this space where she was building her future. A future he wasn't sure he had a place in. No matter what the future held, he wanted her to always remember how he loved her in this moment.

Hunter pulled away. "Go lock the front door."

"Hunter," she giggled. "Not here. We can't."

He shoved her against the wall and yanked on her hair, forcing her to look up at him. He crushed his lips against hers, nipping and tugging to indicate his impatience, his need. His knee jammed between hers to pry her legs open while his free hand found its way under her dress to caress her thigh.

"Go lock the damn door," he demanded.

Trembling, she stumbled away to do as he said. Dimly, she heard him radio something about walking her out to his team, but the click of that lock falling into place was so loud that she couldn't be sure. She turned to see him walk to the backdoor and lock it as well. When he turned, she felt rooted to the spot under his predatory gaze as he walked toward her.

"Come."

With her heart racing in her chest, she thought that prey was supposed to run, but found she went straight to her hunter's clutches with that one command.

He captured her in his arms, kissed her as he walked her backward into the bathroom where no one would see. He turned on the light before tugging her dress up.

"Hunter, seriously. Should we be doing this?" She moaned as his fingers pushed her panties aside to caress her. "Oh, gawd. What if someone hears us?"

"You're so fucking wet already," he hissed beside her ear. "Let them hear."

Then he captured her mouth with his, swallowing every moan, every gasp he wrenched from her as he touched and stroked, ruthlessly driving her up and up. Barely balancing on the edge of the vanity, she held on to him, fearing she might literally fall as she teetered on the edge of her orgasm.

As she shattered, he broke their kiss to let her wails of pleasure fill the small room.

"I hope they heard that," he said darkly, kissing her neck again. "Take this off. I want another to make sure they did."

Released from his hold, Gianna leaned heavily against the vanity. She stared at him and tried to recover her sanity.

"I don't think…"

She trailed off as he pushed his shorts and boxers down.

"Did you have something to say?" Hunter asked, drawing her attention further as he stroked his cock. "Take it off, Gianna."

Her breath hitched and her thighs clinched together as she obeyed, unable to stop what she so desperately wanted. The heat in his eyes, his demanding touch washed away all her fears and doubts. How could there be anything wrong between them when his desire for her was like a tangible, living thing?

She could only give in. But the moment she dropped the dress to the floor, he turned her and pressed behind her. Panicked, she tried to push away.

"Hunter, wait—"

"No," he whispered against her ear. He gripped her chin to turn her face so that their eyes met in the mirror. "Watch me fuck you, Gianna. You have more power here than you think."

Her chest heaved as she stared at him. This was a position they had never tried, borne from a fear she hadn't quite overcome since her assault. He never pushed for it before, but for some reason, he couldn't let it go this time. He needed this as a pathetic consolation prize when what he really needed as her love.

"Watch me," he repeated before trailing hungry kisses down her neck and across her shoulder.

There was a wildness to his eyes, one she was certain matched her own. Shouldn't she have felt fear? But as he tugged her breast from her bra to pluck her nipple, she realized she felt anything but. She moaned in pleasure and his movements became even more desperate.

"You're so fucking hot. So goddamn beautiful. And mine. You're mine. Say 'I'm yours.' Say it," he demanded, pushing her forward so he could rub the tip of his cock against her clit.

Gianna moaned again. "I'm yours."

"Take it," he said, slamming inside her.

Enthralled, she watched him in the mirror as she did just that. Watched him as hands roamed her body, touching and caressing her as if she was the holy grail. Watched as he responded to the sounds she made, changing his pace to draw out her pleasure. In that moment, she truly understood what he meant. She *did* have power. She *did* have control.

Bent over the bathroom counter, their sounds of ecstasy created an erotic song to the rhythmic beat of flesh striking flesh. Seizing control, she pressed her hips back to meet him thrust for thrust. She cried out his name, demanded more. Yes, there was control here, and a power so sweet and potent that she felt it vibrating along every inch of her skin.

As they came, she swore that she would only use that power to keep them together like this. Forever.

∞∞∞∞∞∞

They moved into the basement unit that weekend, handling the bulk of the set up in just two days. While London and Tony built a four-door console, Jun and Hunter mounted their TV on the wall. Ciara handled the bathroom while Emilia and Sam built a second console in the bedroom. Valerie and Gianna unpacked the kitchen items that had been in her condo. All that remained were the modular couches that would be delivered in the near future.

Gianna had refused to set up the bathroom, too embarrassed to be in there with everyone in the house. It was bad enough that Hunter had been there as well, sending her not so subtle and suggestive glances. Knowing exactly what he had done to her in there. The man had looked more pleased than their cats after receiving a treat.

She did it again. Referred to something as *theirs* again. She remembered how surprised, how terrified she had been the first time she realized what she had done. Standing in that kitchen, butterflies fluttering in her stomach and around her heart. Now, a week later, she couldn't count how many times she had referred to something as *theirs*. Hers and Hunter's.

She had come to accept that she was in love with

him, but this joint ownership felt different now. This his and hers feeling now nestled quietly in her heart where it bloomed into a deeper love than she thought was possible.

Now, alone in her future tutoring space, Gianna organized some of her math manipulatives and teaching aids into the living room console. After the way he took her in the bathroom, her concerns regarding the distance she had felt growing between them were assuaged. Now she wondered when would be the best time to confess her love.

The last week had been so hectic. She wanted to be alone to figure out what she would do. So, she convinced Hunter to use his day off to rest rather than join her. Though he worked most Saturdays, his younger sister, Naomi, was the one needed on site today.

They passed the plumbing and electrical inspection on Monday and had spent the remainder of the work week closing up the walls, and, led by Naomi's team, installed flooring. She could hear them above her every now and then as they finished what they hadn't yesterday. Naomi hoped to finish tiling the bathrooms today too.

And so, the punch list was getting smaller and smaller. Her move in date coming closer and closer.

She wanted him to move in with her, into this place that was now as much hers as it was his. Theirs. But how could she ask him to give up his place? One that he had purchased and renovated to his liking? It was too fast, too soon. Logically, Gianna understood this. She should just move in to her place, and let their relationship play out until they both confessed their love.

But she didn't want to wait. She wanted to start their lives together as soon as he handed her the keys.

She jumped in surprise at the sudden, aggressive banging on her door. Annoyed, she pushed to her feet, wondering who the hell was banging on her door like she owed them money. As she turned, she saw a silhouette framed by the afternoon light at the backdoor. She stopped walking, her stomach tightening, when she heard the handle turn.

"Gianna?" a somewhat familiar voice called. "Are you in there?"

She stepped closer, trying to place that voice and finally got a better glimpse of him when he looked over his shoulder.

"Todd? What are you doing here?"

"I want to talk to you. I've been trying to talk to you," he said, clearly annoyed. He turned the door handle again. "Open the door."

"Yeah, I'm not going to do that," she assured him, her instincts going haywire. "You need to leave."

"Why are you like this? You keep brushing me off like I don't exist one day and then smiling and flirting with me the next."

"Todd, I'm telling you to leave. You're not listening so I'm going to call the police." Gianna picked up her phone and held the buttons on the side until the Emergency SOS appeared on her phone.

"Don't!" He slapped the door, surprising another jolt from her. "Just open the door, and I'll make you feel really good like the little whore you are. I heard you down here last week, you know. When I didn't see Hunter walk you out like he said he was doing, I came down here only to hear you panting like slut. You put out for Hunter but you can't for me?"

When the dispatcher connected, she didn't hesitate, and spoke even louder so that he could hear and know that she wasn't lying.

"There is a man trying to break into my home."

But instead of scaring him off, this only further enraged Todd. As she continued speaking to the dispatcher, he retrieved a hammer from his toolbelt and hit the glass. As a contractor, he knew exactly where to strike, how much force to use, and it wasn't long before the glass began splintering.

She was yelling her address when the glass shattered completely. The crack exploded like a gunshot as shards rained down. He reached through to turn the lock and shoved the door open.

Stupid, she thought. She was so stupid for not leaving when she had the chance, but she had been so sure that he would leave. With people upstairs and the police on the phone, why couldn't that have been enough of a deterrence? It was the last thought she had before she saw him raise the hammer over his head. It was too late to stop him from swinging, but not too late to move.

The hammer gleamed for a split second in the dim light, arching toward her head with all the clumsy force he could muster. His feet were planted too wide, his hips stiff. He was swinging like it was a sledgehammer and she was drywall. Moving on trained instinct, she stepped in, not away. Fear surged up her spine, then flattened into something sharper, colder. Her body knew what to do, even if her mind hadn't caught up.

Both arms came up hard, stopping his wrist between hers and swept up with a rooftop block to force his swing away. The hammer missed her head by inches. If he had lost his grip, it would have fallen on her. But while he wasn't expecting resistance, his grip remained firm in his belief that size was all he needed to take her.

Her right hand snapped forward in the next breath, the heel of her palm slamming into his nose. There was a chilling cracking sound as blood spurted out and his head jerked back. He staggered, off-balance, shocked and in pain.

Going in for the kill, she didn't give him the chance to recover. Her knee chambered sharply, and she drove a front kick straight into his gut. His breath escaped in a wheeze as he folded slightly at the waist and slammed into the wall.

She stepped forward and seized his wrist. She bent forward and twisted, pulling him off his feet with a movement that was half muscle, half gravity. They tumbled to the ground, her body riding the motion like a practiced fall. The hammer slipped from his fingers and skittered out of reach.

Gianna landed on top, her knee pinning his ribs, and her other foot planted solidly beside his body. He suddenly recovered the wherewithal to struggle, but it was useless now. She pinned his hand between her shoulder and neck before placing both hands on the back of his elbow. She pressed and his arm moved in the opposite direction it should.

"Ow! You bitch! You fucking whore! You're breaking my arm!"

Livid, she glared down at him. "Shut the fuck up, you sorry sack of shit, or I *will* break it. If the police aren't here in the next thirty fucking seconds, I'll have you wishing that the only thing I broke was your stupid fucking nose and arm."

Her heart thundered, her breath short and sharp in

her throat. In the distance, someone was shouting. Footsteps echoed, getting closer. She didn't move. She wouldn't.

"Gianna," Eddie pleaded gently. "Let us—"

"The only way he gets off this fucking floor is with a broken arm or in police cuffs," she snarled.

They didn't argue, and fortunately didn't have to as Naomi opened the door to the police. As promised, Gianna released him when only when she heard the satisfying click of hand cuffs locking around his wrists. The moment she released him, her body felt immediately heavy. She swayed, nearly falling before Naomi and Eddie caught her.

They helped her outside to sit on the stairs leading up to the two homes she would soon move into. She stared blankly at the ground, unable to speak, unwilling to feel. It was only after her sister arrived and cradled her in her arms that she shattered like the glass that now littered the floor of her own home.

∞∞∞∞∞∞∞∞

A thousand different scenarios went through his head after he received his sister's call. Naomi had been annoyingly sparse on the details, telling him only that he needed to quickly get to Johnson-Maffucci site for an emergency. As directed, he parked in the back and found his sister waiting for him in the garage.

"We have to go through the side door to the front porch," she said, leading him.

"What happened, Naomi?" He didn't like how so serious she was being.

"First, you need to know that she's okay. She handled it. Very well actually. So please don't panic, okay?"

"She?" He asked, a spark of fear igniting in his belly.

He looked across the small backyard to the backdoor of Gianna's basement where he knew she worked. His eyes flew open when he saw the police officer, the door empty of glass. Before he could rush over, Naomi jumped in front of him.

"Don't! They're still... we can't go in. She's up front. She's fine. This is the worst of it."

"*What's* the worst of it? Why didn't she call me? What happened?" He demanded, striding to the front of the house as he spoke.

"Todd," she whispered.

He stopped abruptly. Of the thousand scenarios he pictured, this one had never crossed his mind. Enraged, he raced inside and caught the tail end of the questioning as he stepped out onto the porch.

"He's saying that you kept coming by to flirt with him," the officer shared.

Gianna leaned forward, resting her elbows on her knees to rub her temples. "My sister and I are renovating this home to live in. We both come by a few times a month to speak with the construction manager and see the progress. We both have cordial, professional conversations with everyone on the construction crew."

The officer made a note. "And the donuts?"

"Donuts?" She asked, genuinely confused.

"He says you frequently brought him his favorite donuts."

Gianna laughed, both angry and amused. There was just no fucking way to win with some men.

"*We*," she said, pointing to herself and Emilia. "Brought three dozen glazed donuts to the site for the entire crew about once a month. All glazed, no other flavors or types that would create any issues with the crew if their favorite or preferred donut was taken by someone else. And to ensure that there would be no leftovers. *Everyone* eats glazed donuts, whether they're a favorite or not."

"Are you done?" Hunter called angrily as he came down the steps. "You're questioning her as though that piece of shit you have in the car is the victim."

"And who are you?"

"Hunter Hall, construction manager and Todd's *former* employer."

He went to Gianna's side, grateful when Emilia made space for his own arm to go around her shoulders. She looked up at him briefly, her eyes still slightly puffy and red from crying. There were droplets of blood splattered on her shirt. He didn't know who it belonged too, but he immediately wanted to beat Todd. If he wasn't already inside of the police car, his dead body would be inside Hunter's trunk.

"Have you had any issues of this type with Todd in the past?"

Hunter shook his head. "No, not in the time that he's been employed with me. But he has had a restraining order for harassing clients at his previous place of employment."

"What?" Emilia shouted, shoving Hunter's hand away. "How could you hire someone like that? This is basically your fault."

"I—"

Hunter didn't know what to say. He looked at Gianna with haunted eyes. She started to reach for him just as her sister pulled her to her feet.

"Wait—" she started to say.

"Can we leave now?' Emilia demanded. "Hasn't she been through enough already?"

"I think we have all we need," the officer replied. "You're free to go."

"But—" Gianna protested.

She was cut off when Emilia led her away. Hunter still didn't speak. Instead, he turned and looked back at the house, knowing he didn't deserve to be with her.

"It's not your fault, Hunter," Naomi said gently.

Hunter sighed in disagreement. "Can you catch up to Emilia and see if she'll let you and Trevor get Gianna's car home? I don't want her to have to come back here tomorrow."

"Right, okay," she said and chased after Emilia.

"Eddie—"

"She kicked his ass. We had to keep her from breaking his arm. Right, Jose?"

"We?" Jose snorted. "Nah, not we. I wanted her to break his arm. Fucking asshole."

"That's not what I was going to ask," Hunter chuckled, though he did feel some of the tension leave his body. "But, thanks for telling me. I needed to hear that. I need you to run up to the hardware store for some boards for the door. And new locks for all of the doors. I'll authorize your overtime so we can get everything changed tonight. Once I get inside, I'll call you to see if we need anything else. You know how to charge it to the corporate account?"

"Yeah, I got it," Eddie said. "But don't worry about the OT. I know we have no choice but to eat the costs to repair and replace everything, but that fucker isn't about to cost us more in payroll. At least that's how I feel about it."

Jose nodded in agreement when Eddie looked over at him. "I'm here 'till we get it done. It's the least we can do."

Grateful, Hunter let them go and got on the phone to try to get a new door rush ordered. The cops took another forty-five minutes to collect evidence and clear the scene. With them gone, he knew he couldn't put it off any longer.

Hunter sucked in a deep breath and let himself in the front door. He glanced around the room, pictured her sitting in front of the storage console. It was still open and there were still boxes on the floor. In the kitchen, shards of glass were scattered all over the floor. Dark red blood was splattered along the dented wall and on the floor. One of the barstools had been knocked over in the fight that had ensued. Had her heart hammered in her chest this same way? While he was filled with rage, had she been filled with fear?

Had she considered, even for a moment, calling him?

"Don't do this to yourself, Hunter. Don't make this about you," he reminded himself.

But as he retrieved the broom from the small closet across from the bathroom, his thoughts tumbled out uncontrollably. He swept himself deeper into despair, into depression, as he swept up the shards of glass.

He had no way to vent his anger, no way to heal this hurt. He couldn't even go to her like he wanted because even though he knew exactly where she was, even though he knew Emilia didn't want him there, he didn't have her sister's address. Weeks earlier this would have bothered him, but now he felt like he didn't deserve to have this information.

Todd had always been toxic, had always taken more than he gave. It was only out of misplaced pity that he hired him in the first place. His skills at the time had been barely average, but he had patiently guided him along. Todd's life, no matter how pitiful, was the product of his own actions and if he didn't have the sense to get out of his own way, there was nothing he could do about it.

He should have ended his friendship with him years ago. If he had, Todd would never have met Gianna. Would never have been here, and she would have never been in danger. This whole thing was his fault.

The realization came too late. Todd was out of the picture and took with him the hope that Gianna actually needed him.

CHAPTER 15

Gianna didn't make it back to the basement all week. It wasn't from a lack of trying on her part. She was certain her family and friends were conspiring to keep her away. Though each of them had a different reason or excuse that didn't appear to tie together, she was still suspicious nonetheless.

Hunter's reasons were the only ones that seemed plausible. With Todd off the job, there was one less man to do the work and only a week and a half to get everything done. They were all picking up extra responsibilities, which now included fixing the damage that Todd had caused. As a result, Hunter went home feeling too exhausted for more than a brief telephone conversation.

He wouldn't even let her come over to keep him company. Here she was, full of love, and the guy was too damn exhausted from building her dream house. Was it any wonder she wanted to take their relationship to the next level so quickly?

She tried to curb her annoyance as she hunted for a parking space, though it was honestly getting more difficult each day. The rest of her family and friends insisted that she wait until the weekend when they were free to join her, but she was unwilling to wait that long.

No matter how she many times she reassured them that she was fine, she felt like none of them took her seriously. Maybe she should have broken the guy's arm after all. It might have provided that missing piece of reassurance and comfort that they all seemed to need.

Well, she circumvented all of them by reaching out to Naomi for her new set of keys. She wanted to finish setting up her materials, and, more importantly, she needed to get back in that space and prove to everyone that she wasn't afraid. There were Todds everywhere in the world, and she hadn't spent years of martial arts training to cower in bed for the rest of her life.

She parked a block away and walked to her house. By the time she arrived, she was sweating. She couldn't imagine the crew working much longer in his heat. When she arrived, she found Hunter standing at the bottom of the stairs.

Her heart tripped as she drunk in the sight of him. The tank he wore was darkened by sweat and his arms, thinly coated in sweat as well, glistened in the sun. The hair that covered his chin and lips told her that he had gone yet another week without touching up his goatee. He didn't wear his usual toolbelt, but the pockets of his cargo pants appeared full to the brim.

Their eyes met when she stopped at the iron gate surrounding her home. Behind those beautiful, brown eyes was a softness and an exhaustion she had never seen before. Concerned, she pulled open the gate and crossed to him. Throwing her arms around his neck, she squeezed him tight.

"I missed you."

His heart stuttered as he breathed her in. "I missed you too."

"You wouldn't let me come over," she said, pouting as she pulled back to look up at him. She cupped his cheek. "You look beat."

"I am beat," he smiled weakly in agreement. "But it's almost done. Your house will be done and you can get back to the life you had before all of this."

Gianna didn't know why, but the way he said that bothered her. He led her to the basement unit while she tried to figure out why.

"I don't want you to work yourself to death for us."

"It's fine," he said. He opened the door and led her inside. "We just installed the new door yesterday. I'm sorry it took so long."

"It's fine," she reassured him.

Gianna looked around the room. Stared at the new door. She pictured the floor as it had been that day. She tried to bring back what she felt, but couldn't. There was no anger, no fear. All she felt was love for Hunter and a growing sense of unease.

"You should be able to take a break this weekend, right? I'll come over, bring food so we don't have to cook or clean. Shrek and Fiona probably need more food and cat litter too."

She took his hand, trying to close the distance between them. He held her hand in return and relief washed over her.

"We'll see," he said. He placed the keys in her hand. "Can you give Emilia and Sam their keys as well? Red ones are hers and green are yours."

She blinked when he took a step back. Relief was

replaced with dread.

"Okay," she said, drawing out the word in confusion.

"I need to get back to work. I'll call you tonight."

And then he was gone, leaving her frowning after him. Her eyes watered, but she forced back the tears. He hadn't even kissed her. There was no more imagining the distance between them. No more denying that there wasn't something very wrong here. It had seemed better. But ever since the whole thing with Todd…

Her thoughts trailed off as she considered the time. Did he think she had actually led him on? That something had happened between them that led to him attacking her?

Her breath hitched and a solitary tear slipped out. Panicking, she angrily swiped it away. She wouldn't think that. *Couldn't.* There had to be another reason. They had come too far, grown too much together for him to still see her as the girl those rumors had made her out to be.

Whatever it was, he didn't want to talk about it.

"Idiot," she muttered. "I'm in love with an idiot."

She went out the backdoor, following him into the backyard. What was left of their backyard after the expansion was just under 800 square feet of usable space. They had cleared it since she was last here and so she was able to see him across the yard as he made his way into the garage.

"Hunter!" She called, her voice commanding him to stop.

He stopped mid-stride and turned to face her, brows lifting in surprise. "Forget something?"

She walked to him, her strides determined. "I want

to know what's going on with you."

He blinked. "Going on with what?"

"With you," she said, stepping closer. "You've been off for months. Distant. Different."

"I've just been tired," he replied, too quickly. "Working on *your* house, Gianna."

Her eyes narrowed. "There. That. Why did you say it like that? Why put so much weight on 'your'? What are you really trying to say?"

He sighed and glanced up at the house. "Can we not do this here? Just come over this weekend like you said, and we'll talk then."

"No," she said, shaking her head, voice rising. "We agreed that we would share what we're feeling, remember? But you haven't been doing that, have you? So, tell me, what's been running through your head? What conclusions have you jumped to this time?"

"I'm not jumping to any conclusions," he said stiffly, even though he had done exactly that more times than he cared to count.

She took a breath, her hands balling into fists at her sides. "I'm going to kick your ass if you stand there and try to gaslight me. I know what I feel. You've been cold. You've been pulling away. You didn't even kiss me goodbye just now. You're being a coward and running away again and I demand to know why."

"I can't run from something that is probably about to end," he said defensively.

She stared at him. "You're going to want to say that one more fucking time. And explain to me, like I'm as stupid as you are, why you think that."

"Come on, Gianna. Be real. I'm not the only one holding back. I'm not the only one being distant. You've kept our worlds and the people in it separated quite neatly this whole time. You and me? We're together. But yours and mine? Never the two shall meet. If my siblings didn't work for Hall Construction, you would never try to meet them. And how many family dinners have you invited me to?"

"You're right," she agreed. "Keep going. Get it all out."

Annoyed by her easy admission of guilt, he continued. "How many plans have you made about this house? A house that I've poured my blood and sweat into that won't include me after I hand over the keys? This is your house. Yours. Every day we get closer to finishing, I worry that it'll be the end of us instead of the beginning that I want. How can I not pull away?"

She stared at him blankly, waiting for him to continue. For some reason, it upset him even more.

"When you didn't even think to call me after that shit with Todd, I was sure that that you don't even factor me into your big picture. That man tried to hurt you and it never crossed your mind to let your boyfriend know that you had almost been hurt. Worse, I couldn't check on you because I don't have Emilia's address. Do you know how fucking demoralizing that is? I know that you're strong, that you can take care of yourself. But damn, Gianna, I want to take care of you too."

Not knowing what else to say, and having said entirely too much, he fell silent and looked down at her feet. It was a moment before she spoke.

"Are you in love with me, Hunter?"

His head snapped up. Wide eyed, he stared at her. Her eyes, seemingly all knowing, pierced through him as she waited patiently for a response.

He didn't want to tell her. Not like this. Even though he wasn't sure where this was heading, he still felt that she deserved romance when he told her.

"Nothing to say? Even now. I wonder why you have to be backed into a corner to admit you feelings. Whatever. It's fine. It's better that I provide an answer to all my crimes first. It might change how you feel about me."

"It's not like—"

Gianna held her hand up to stop him. "It's my turn now. First, you're right. I have been holding back, hiding that last piece of me by keeping our most close circles separate. It wasn't my intention, but I acknowledge that the impact of that behavior still hurt you. I'm sorry for that. London and Valerie pointed it out a few weeks ago and I had planned to invite you to my next family dinner to remedy this."

"I—"

"Second," she continued, speaking over him. "I have made many plans for this house, but halfway through the renovations, it stopped feeling like it was just my project. I may have picked out the fixtures and appliances and cabinets and what have you. But my half of the house? I've left all the walls white. Do you know why?"

He shrugged. "Maybe you weren't ready to pick a color."

"No. I wasn't. I wasn't because I started envisioning painting them with the man I loved so that it would our space and not just mine."

Those words hit him like a brick, leaving him momentarily dazed. Before he could recover to respond, she continued speaking.

"As for my third crime, I'm wondering if you

understand the SOS feature on your phone. As a man, it's existence probably doesn't even cross your mind. But for me, it's quite literally a matter of life and death."

She retrieved her phone from her pocket and held it out to him.

"With the press of these buttons, I can quickly get patched through to emergency services. My phone also automatically sends an SOS message to anyone listed as an emergency contact in my phone. This may come as a surprise to you," she said dryly, "But even though we've been dating for eight months now, I haven't added you as an emergency contact yet. Do you have me listed as yours? Of course you don't. By the time the police and Emilia arrived, you were also already here. Between falling apart and getting questioned by the police, no, it didn't occur to me to call you. Shocker, right?"

She tried to laugh, but sound that escape her lips was something between a chuckle and an agonized groan.

"I'm still new to this. Still learning. As tutors, we know better than anyone that learning and improving requires guidance. Instruction. Patience. I'm not saying you have to be responsible for my growth, but if I was doing something to hurt you, why didn't you tell me? If you had, I would have found a way to learn how to be better. If you really loved me, wouldn't you have given me a chance to be better instead of pulling away?"

"I..." he trailed off, not knowing what to say.

She shook her head sadly. "I love you, Hunter. I have for a while. It just seemed too soon to tell you."

The words washed over him and poured into his heart to fill it to the brim. He reached for her, unsurprised when she took a step back. He dropped his hand and stared at her.

"If you really love me, why do you keep pulling away? You keep levelling me with your insecurities, your need to be control, every time something doesn't go your way. That's not the kind of relationship I want to be in. Where do we go from here? How do I get you to trust my heart? To trust yours?"

"I'm sorry, Gianna. I just feel…I just love you so much. I can't think straight."

"Then let's take some time until you can."

She turned and walked away.

"Gianna," he called, rushing to catch up to her. "Gianna, wait."

She heard his footsteps behind her before she felt the pressure of his hand, but she didn't stop walking. His grip tightened, not painful, but insistent. She stopped at the backdoor to the basement unit, suddenly feeling light headed from trying to stop herself from falling apart. She just needed a moment. Just a moment to get it together.

"Please stop touching me," she said softly, still facing away.

"Don't leave," he demanded quietly, stepping closer. "Let's talk about this."

"I think we've said enough today. We're both feeling a lot right now," she said, staring at his reflection through the glass door. "Let's give each other some space to sort through it and have a conversation when we're both calm."

Judging from her voice, he was the only one spiraling. Her level of calm terrified him. She didn't have a reason to walk away from him before, but he had given her plenty. Inadvertently, his grip tightened.

If he let her walk away now, he feared this really would be the end of them.

"You're hurting my arm, Hunter."

The moment he released her arm she quickly stepped forward, opening the door and dashing inside. He reached for her just as the door shut in his face. The lock slid into place soon after.

"Gianna!" he shouted.

But she was already walking away.

∞∞∞∞∞∞∞

A week and a half passed. Hunter called her every day, no matter how late it was when he returned home from work. Most times, she answered or returned his calls. They only ever spoke briefly, and their interactions were nothing like they had always been. Gone was the playful banter, the suggestive innuendos.

Instead, she kindly acknowledged and dismissed him at the same time, informing him that she was swamped with multiple competing priorities. At work, she also had projects to close out, some of which included UI glitches that took up a lot of her time to repair. It all needed to be done before she took time off work to move in. He knew she planned to join Emilia and Sam on their final visit with the child they were hoping to adopt next week. They also had to coordinate movers not only for Emilia's place, but for Gianna's storage unit as well.

He knew it was selfish to want their love to be the main priority, especially right now. But since it wasn't, he worried that they had completely fucked up their chance for a solid relationship. How stupid they had both been for failing to be honest about their feelings when it mattered most.

Sighing, Hunter parked in his driveway, physically and emotionally exhausted. As much as he wanted to rush over and fix it all, he knew the timing wasn't right. He chose instead to believe that this wouldn't be the end of them. Chose to believe that she loved him as deeply as he loved her.

He dragged himself from the car. He had been at a new jobsite all day, unable to get away to check on Gianna. Escrow had closed on Gianna's property that morning and Madison had given them the keys today in his stead. Jose and Eddie had called out sick due to food poisoning, so he had been stuck filling in for them. He felt a sense of dread having missed the opportunity to see her take her first steps inside her new home. In hindsight though, it was probably for the best that he hadn't been able to get away. Who knows how he would have reacted to seeing her.

As he approached his door, Hunter immediately noticed the white piece of paper with boldly written red words that read "DON'T PANIC" taped to it. He recognized the handwriting as Gianna's and unlocked the door. She still had the key to his place. Had she snuck in and taken her cats back? She really didn't want to see him. The thought was like a punch to the gut.

But when he flicked on the lights, he found that his living room was bare.

He blinked in confusion as he stared. His couch, tv, entertainment system, and all that it held was missing. The cat tree that had stood in the corner was also missing. Walking into the kitchen, he opened cabinets, but found everything in its place. The only thing missing from there were cat food items. The dining table was still in its place and absolutely nothing had been touched in either of the two bedrooms.

Hunter scratched his head, unsure if he should feel panicked, despite what the sign had said. Had she taken her cats and accidently left the door unlocked, allowing someone to sneak in behind her and rob him? Considering the neat state of his place, however, and the sign on the door, it was more likely that she had let someone take his things. But that didn't make sense either.

He lifted his phone to call Gianna just as a message from her came through, telling him to come to her house. His heart thudded in his chest before he turned on his heel to head out the door. The issue of his empty living room forgotten, he barely remembered to lock up.

Traffic had started to clear up on his drive home and was even more so now. It didn't take him long to get to Gianna's, but he did spend what felt like hours hunting for a parking space. He didn't know why she wanted to see him, but he hoped it meant that she was ready to talk. Ready to fix this between them so that they could explore this love together.

As instructed, he rang the doorbell for Emilia's. As if she had been waiting for him, she appeared in an instant. Throwing herself into his arms, she kissed him noisily.

"Hi! Bleh, you stink!"

Shocked by this friendly greeting, Hunter held her a moment, wondering if he was dreaming. It took him a minute to realize that she was already dragging him inside.

"You too," he murmured, trying to play it as cool as

she was. "I was knocking down walls today. How much have you been unpacking already to be this sweaty?"

"Poor planning on our part for sure," she explained as she dragged him in. "But we couldn't find Zia's picture. It was supposed to go in Emilia's car but ended up on the truck. So. It's been a day."

He paused with Gianna in front of a maple-colored console table. Mounted on the wall above the console was a large portrait of a woman in her late sixties with silver-streaked chestnut hair swept into an elegant chignon. Her olive skin bore fine lines like delicate etchings of a well-lived life, and her dark eyes, still fierce with vitality, held warmth that immediately made him feel welcome.

On the console itself were various framed photos. Though most of them were of Emilia, Sam, and Ciara, some included Gianna and the woman he assumed was their aunt. But it was the photo sitting in the center of them all that captured his attention and made his heart race.

It was a photo of him and Gianna in bright life vests and dark sunglasses as they paddle boarded on Lake Natoma a few months ago. Located between Folsom and Nimbus Dam, the small lake was part of the Folsom Lake State Recreation Area. They had so much fun that day discovering another activity unique to the Sacramento area that they had never really taken advantage of before.

Hunter looked over at her to find her staring at the photo on the wall, a pleased smile on her face.

"Zia, this is my future husband, Benjamin Hunter Hall III. Even though he's kind of an idiot for thinking I don't want to be with him forever, I still love the guy. Anyway, we haven't actually settled on all of that stuff yet, but you always said it's better to get forgiveness later and take what you want first."

His heart lodged in his throat, preventing him from speaking. He could only stare at her wide eyed.

"That is *not* what she said, Gianna!" Emilia called loudly from further inside.

"Pretty sure she did," Gianna insisted as she took his hand and guided him into the kitchen.

Emilia, Sam, and Ciara sat on the floor around two boxes. On it was an opened box of pepperoni pizza. They didn't bother with plates as they picked up slices to eat.

"The correct saying is 'It's better to beg for forgiveness than to ask for permission,' if that is what you meant," Sam explained. "Hi, Hunter."

"Hi…" he said, still dazed.

Gianna snorted and pulled Hunter down to the floor to sit beside her. She dropped a napkin in his lap and picked up a slice of pizza.

"I'm not asking permission to marry him," she said around a bite. "I'm *telling* him. He likes it when I'm bossy. Right, Hunter?"

"There are minors in the room," Emilia reminded her when Gianna sent Hunter a saucy wink. "Hunter, now that you're going to be a part of this family, I really need you to do a better job of keeping your future wife in check."

"I…" he trailed off, then stared at her. "Gianna…"

He stood and pulled her up with him, taking her pizza and tossing it back in the box before she could take another bite.

"Hey! My pizza!"

Ignoring her, he dragged her outside.

"Gianna… what is this? I thought… When you left

you said…" He honestly couldn't get his thoughts straight.

Gianna looked up at him, saw the confused pain in his eyes. She placed her hands on his chest.

"Oh, no. What did I say wrong this time? Why did you think I was breaking up with you?"

Hunter stepped forward and pulled her into his arms. He pressed his lips to her forehead and just breathed there a moment until he was ready to speak.

"Asking for space in a relationship is usually considered the first red flag before a break up," he informed her.

"You've got to be kidding me. That's not what I meant. I was just feeling a little hurt and a lot mad and wanted to be alone for a bit. Besides, it's not like I stopped talking to you! I've been telling you my plans all week."

"Yes, but, I'm… an idiot," he admitted, clinging to her now out of sheer embarrassment.

Gianna rolled her eyes. "If that wasn't established before. Well, at least I know I didn't go too far. Clearly you need a big gesture to actually trust that I'm all in."

He pulled back enough to look into her eyes. "I'm sorry."

"The only apology either of us should accept is changed behavior. Let me show you mine."

She pulled him across the porch, leading him to her door. Then she pointed to the keypad lock on it.

"Code is your birthday and mine," she told him, pushing him toward the door. "Open it up."

"Gianna—"

"Inside first, Hunter," she insisted.

He let out a resigned sigh before putting in the code and opening the door. It was dark as they stepped inside and since he was worried about tripping over boxes, he didn't go far. Then Gianna turned on the light and after he saw what was inside, he remained rooted in place, unable to move even if he wanted to.

"Welcome home," she said quietly behind him.

Though boxes were stacked along every wall, one room was already set up. In the middle of the living room, two mismatched couches faced each other. One was her own cozy white couch and the other was the one missing tattered gray couch from his living room. Sitting against the wall between them was his entertainment center, television, and game systems.

"How?" He asked as he continued to look around.

"Jose and Eddie. They weren't really sick today," she said, smiling as she stepped up to stand beside him.

"Why?" he whispered.

"I love you, Hunter. Love is complicated and hard. It's messy. You're going to make me mad, and I'm going to drive you crazy. I'm going to say the wrong thing and you'll jump to the wrong conclusions. But even still, the love will always be worth it."

Hunter turned to face her. Their eyes locked and everything else fell away. When their lips finally met, it felt as if they had been waiting lifetimes to find each other again. The kiss deepened, fierce and slow, tasting of longing, of questions answered without words.

But he knew that the words, and so much more, needed to be said.

Hunter pulled away, held her face between his hands. "I love you so fucking much."

"Prove it," she said with a grin. "Move in with me."

"Are you—" He stopped himself before he could question her. He couldn't do that anymore. He would forever trust in this woman from here on out. "Say it again."

"Ugh. So bossy," she said with a mock sigh and a roll of her eyes, though her heart beat with wild excitement. "I love you, Hunter. Now are you moving in or what?"

"Or what first," he said, and pulled her in for another searing kiss.

Gianna chuckled as he walked her backward toward the couch, his lips moving to her neck.

"Shouldn't we talk more?" she questioned, sliding her hands up his chest to gently push him away. "We're kind of a mess, you and I."

He nodded in agreement. "And yet you still want me. I'm sorry I didn't trust that you did. I'm sorry that I didn't tell you I loved you sooner. I promise to let you kick my ass if I ever forget to be patient because we're both learning how to love."

She placed a gentle hand on his cheek, smiling up at him with eyes that were full of love.

"I'm sorry that I didn't tell you that sooner, that I didn't let you in sooner. I promise to continue learning and growing so that not a day goes by where you question how much I love you."

"We'll both be better," he said, kissing her softly. "Together."

Gianna grinned against his lips. "Good. Now, let's head back next door."

"Gianna," he said, grabbing her ass. He eyed the couch. "Take pity on me."

"Sorry, babe. You're going to have to suck it up," she insisted, leading him out of the house. "It's the first Wednesday of the month. Family dinner night. You can't miss your first one."

Hunter squeezed her hand. "Okay."

He let her take him back inside Emilia's house. They joined them on the floor. Surrounded by boxes and the warm noise of familiar voices, Hunter took in the faces around him. The laughter, the teasing, the easy closeness. The bond this family shared and strengthened every first Wednesday of the month, seemed to stretch and shift to make room for him.

Gianna leaned into Hunter, her hand resting lightly on his thigh. He captured it without hesitation, threading his fingers through hers. She glanced up at him, and when he smiled, something in her finally settled. For the first time in a long time, she didn't just hope love was worth it. She knew it was.

EPILOGUE

Bright white canopies stretched the length of the two yards, casting cool, fluttering shadows over the patchwork of green grass between the two houses. Overhead, misters hissed a steady wet mist into the air, their fine spray catching the sunlight like a halo and caressing everyone with a refreshing, nearly invisible veil of coolness.

Laughter rose and fell like waves, blending seamlessly with the thump of old-school R&B and classic rock tunes humming from a wireless speaker perched on a table near the grill. The scent of sizzling meats danced through the air, drawing guests in lazy procession toward the food table like bees to blossoms.

Beneath the canopies, rows of folding tables dressed in alternating blue and white cloths bore the weight of bowls and plates, cups, and cans, some empty and some full. There was enough seating for at least thirty people, and half the chairs were already full.

A few more guests wandered in through the side gate, greeted with cheers and hugs as they joined the celebration.

Though the forecast promised a scorching Memorial Day afternoon edging near a hundred degrees, no one seemed to mind. The misters kept their skin dewy and the shade gave them comfort while they filled their bellies and enjoyed each other's company.

"I know you're being serious right now, but you do realize how crazy this idea is, right?"

Gianna propped her hand under her elbow as she thought about it, her eyes far away. Then she looked at Hunter.

"Nope. It still makes perfect sense to me."

Valerie grinned at her. "I actually kind of love the idea."

"You've got to be kidding me. You used to be the reasonable one," Hunter reminded her.

"See!" Gianna laughed. "We just need to get London on board. London! Get your ass over here!"

"Gianna, we're getting married in two and a half months."

"And?" She slanted him annoyed look. "You insisted on being engaged for a year, not me. Tony and London were only engaged for six months."

"Thank for the reminder to hurt Tony," Hunter said, rolling his eyes.

Tony joined them at the table with another plate covered in food.

"What did I do now?"

Hunter glared at him. "You didn't stay engaged long enough. Now you're about to pay for it. That'll be the only thing I find satisfying about this nonsense."

"Wow, rude. Lots and lots of sex will definitely be

satisfying," Gianna insisted.

"Woah. What did I walk into?" London asked.

"Gianna being Gianna," Valerie explained with a grin. "She has quite the idea for the three of us."

"Oh dear," London said.

"You know her well. Wait, don't say it yet," Hunter said. He held up his hand until he saw Tony take a big bite of food. "Okay. Go."

"I don't see what the big deal is. I just think that since Jun and Valerie are trying to get pregnant then London and I should as well. That way, our kids can be in the same grade like we were."

As Hunter hoped, Tony sputtered and choked on his food. He and Jun rolled with laughter, nearly falling out of their chairs while London comforted her husband. Tony finally recovered to stare in shock at Gianna.

"Are you being serious right now?" He asked.

"She's completely serious. And you're partially to blame," Hunter accused. "You two just had to get married so fast. Now she wants to play catch up. And you. You couldn't wait until after we got married to try making a baby?"

"Ow!" Jun yelped after Hunter punched his shoulder. "Look, you dumbasses have been dragging your feet and fucking up with your women from the start. We've been married for two years now. We're ready."

"So am I!" Gianna leaned into Hunter. "Let's do it! London, are you in? Please be in!"

"Wait, wait, wait," Tony insisted. "We can't—"

"We can," London interrupted. "We *are*, actually."

"London, seriously, we haven't talked about…" He trailed off when she took his hand to place it on her belly.

No one spoke for a full minute.

Tony finally took a shuddering breath. "You're... pregnant?"

"I guess we weren't careful enough when I was on those antibiotics."

"London..." he trailed off before pulling her into his arms. "Oh, fuck. We're going to have a baby?"

"We're going to have a baby," she repeated.

"You're going to have a baby!" Gianna squealed, happy tears already streaming down her face.

"I didn't plan to tell you yet. Thank you," she said to Valerie when she passed her a napkin to dry her tears. "I took the test two days ago so it's still early and you know, anything can happen."

Tony kissed her to silence her. "Let's not worry about that yet. We'll be careful. Oh, fuck."

"Well, shit," Hunter said. "I guess we're all having babies."

Gianna squealed again and jumped into his lap. "Really? You'll do it?"

"I won't survive trying to convince you otherwise."

"Yay! I love you!" She gave him a noisy kiss. "I hope I won't need to alter my wedding dress!"

Jun grinned at her. "You might. You do know twins run in the Hall family, right?"

"Twins?" Gianna squeaked and looked down at Hunter with a shocked expression.

He grinned. "Grandpa Hall was a twin. My mom had twins. You and Valerie could have them too."

"Oh shit."

Valerie laughed. "Don't listen to them. Even if you were pregnant, you won't be showing by then."

"Let's go make some twins now," Hunter said as he

stood with her in his arms. "Better catch up, Jun!"

Jun chuckled. "I might have made mine already this morning."

"Jun!" Valerie chastised.

"What? They're just going to do what we do," he said, wiggling his eyebrows.

"In our house?"

"Oh shit," he blanched before jumping to his feet to chase after them. "Wait!"

249

ABOUT THE AUTHOR

Born and (mostly) raised in Sacramento, California in the 1980s, the world was my oyster. I grew up in a wonderfully culturally diverse neighborhood and as a result, I had a friend from (and a crush on) every ethnic group. And then, thanks to the advent of personal computers and dial up Internet, my world grew even bigger. I spent a lot of time in front of my computer watching anime, chatting on AIM messenger or chat rooms, downloading music from Napster, and writing poetry and fan fiction.

Naturally, this shaped me and kept my mind open and accepting. And love? That was maybe the one thing that was actually colorblind.

But as life would show me over the next several decades, love is a little more nuanced than that. So, with my ever-increasing interest in the written language, I wrote about it. And drawn back to Sacramento, one of America's most diverse cities, I felt the need to dedicate a space that celebrated not only love, but this wonderfully diverse place that no one outside of California seems to know is the capital.

I want you to get to know my city, and maybe, you'll fall in love with the 916 too.

DD DAVIS

#SACRAMENTO

SACRAMENTO, CA

www.visitsacramento.com

Sacramento is the star on the map of California - where you will find cultural attractions to inspire you, cutting-edge cuisine to impress you, history to enrich you and surprises to put a smile on your face. Venture out in any direction and you'll see why we're so fond of saying, "California begins here."

Driving from Sacramento to:
- Napa Valley Wine Country, ~1 hour
- San Francisco, ~1.5 hours
- Lake Tahoe Ski Resorts, ~2 hours
- Yosemite National Park, ~2.5 hours

Flying from Sacramento to:
- Los Angeles, ~1 hour
- Las Vegas, ~ 1.5 hours
- San Diego, ~1.5 hours
- Hawaii, ~5 hours

OLIVE ROSE PHOTOGRAPHY

www.oliverosephotos.com/

We are Jase and Olive, formerly Chasing Olives Photography, a husband and wife partnership since 2016. Why the name change? Just like we have grown and evolved, so has our photography. On-location, outdoor, portrait photography in natural lighting is our favorite because we believe nothing can emulate the magical glow of the sun. We capture memories in Sacramento and Roseville, CA, but that doesn't mean we won't travel for your special occasion. We photograph engagements, families, maternity, graduates, headshots, and pets—just to name a few!

CITY OF TREES

Sacramento was known as the "City of Trees" due to its abundant urban forest and high tree density until 2012. The city has been nicknamed this since the mid-1800s, and it's estimated to have around one million trees within its city limits.

FARM TO FORK CAPITOL

www.visitcalifornia.com/experience/farm-fork-capital/
Sacramento officially became known as "America's Farm-to-Fork Capital" in 2012, when Visit Sacramento and then-Mayor Kevin Johnson promoted the region's agricultural strengths. While the idea was first proposed in 2012, the formal branding and related events like the Farm-to-Fork Festival solidified Sacramento's reputation as a leader in farm-fresh cuisine.

California is undeniably the land of plenty—the largest agricultural producer in the country. And it doesn't get much more rural than the region surrounding Sacramento. This fertile acreage, with remarkable soil and abundant sunshine, means Sacramento has incredible access to the juiciest fruits, freshest vegetables, and an ever-increasing array of artisanal, farm-based products. Area chefs take advantage of the bounty by forming close relationships with farmers and sourcing ingredients that will end up on diners' plates that very same night.

SACRAMENTO KINGS

www.nba.com/kings
The Sacramento Kings are an American professional basketball team.

GOLDEN 1 CENTER

www.golden1center.com
Golden 1 Center sits proudly in the heart of downtown Sacramento, less than a mile from California's first thriving business district.

It's here that you'll find people from all walks of life building a community around their favorite things: Music, sports, entertainment, culture, food, and beverage. A homage to the city's legacy and a marvel of its bright future, Golden 1 Center represents everything that makes Sacramento the next Great American City. From design to sustainability to connectivity to cuisine, it's a celebration of what Sacramento does best.

DOWNTOWN COMMONS (DOCO)

www.docosacramento.com
It's a night on the town with best friends or a seat in the plaza with coffee and a sketchpad. Seeing your favorite band for the first time. Sitting outside in the warm air with a craft cocktail. Surrounding yourself in

amazing art and architecture. Staying at one of the most eclectic hotels in California. Shopping at one-of-a-kind boutiques alongside the most recognized global brands. DOCO is where the locals hang out and visitors from around the globe experience this region at its finest. Sacramento is the next Great American City…and DOCO is our common ground.

DOCO is where the locals hang out and visitors from around the globe experience this region at its finest. Sacramento is the next Great American City and DOCO is our common ground.

DT ROLLER RINK

sacramentorollerrink.com

Downtown Roller Rink is more than just a place to skate—it's a celebration of the dynamic energy and spirit of Sacramento. Whether you're a seasoned skater or lacing up your skates for the first time, our rink offers a welcoming atmosphere for all ages and skill levels.

Join us as we roll into a new era of entertainment and create unforgettable memories right in the heart of downtown Sacramento. See you on the rink!

MIDTOWN

exploremidtown.org

Midtown is the cultural hub of Sacramento, home to a diverse array of housing, businesses, restaurants, bars and shops, with a curated blend of cutting-edge development and historic properties.

CHALK IT UP
chalkitup.org
Chalk It Up To Sacramento aims to empower the next generation of artists by providing grant funding and programs for teachers and schools to give equitable access to the arts for all students, with an emphasis on serving our region's most vulnerable populations. The annual three-day Chalk It Up! Chalk Art & Music Festival, a vibrant celebration of our local arts community and artists of all ages, is offered free to the public over Labor Day weekend, serving as a gift to the city and the greater Sacramento region.

"Chalk It Up to Sacramento It's the Chalk of the Town," better known as Chalk It Up, was first established in 1991 through the hard work of local artists and community art supporters who wanted to bring the transient beauty of Madonnari, the Italian tradition of street painting, to Sacramento. They held the first Chalk It Up Festival at what is now known as Cesar Chavez Park. In 1993, Chalk it Up received its non-profit status and moved the festival to its current home at Fremont Park in Midtown, Sacramento.

SACRAMENTO REGIONAL TRANSIT
www.sacrt.com
The largest regional transit provider in the capital of California.

FAB 40'S
www.visitcalifornia.com/experience/fabulous-forties
In the heart of East Sacramento, bounded by grand

treelined streets, is a residential district renowned not only for its historical significance but also its architectural beauty and community spirit. This is the Fabulous Forties neighborhood, so named because of the numbered avenues it occupies—40th through 49th, between J Street and Folsom Boulevard. While the wider East Sacramento area is prized for its charm and local amenities, the Fabulous Forties stands out as a distinctive and revered enclave.

CALIFORNIA STATE CAPITOL & MUSEUM
www.capitolmuseum.ca.gov
The California State Capitol is the seat of the California government, located in Sacramento, the capital of California. The Capitol building serves as both a museum and the state's working seat of government. The building houses the chambers of the California State Legislature, made up of the California State Assembly and the California State Senate, along with the office of the Governor of California. Visitors to the Capitol can at once experience California's rich history and witness the making of history through the modern lawmaking process.

GREENHAVEN
Pocket-Greenhaven is a suburban community within the city of Sacramento, California, 5 miles south of downtown Sacramento. It is bordered by Interstate 5 on the east and a semi-circular "pocket" bend in the

Sacramento River on the south, west, and north.

DARLING AVIARY

www.darlingaviary.com

At Darling Aviary, located in the heart of Downtown Sacramento, we are committed to sustainable dining and environmental protection. Our innovative menu highlights fresh ingredients sourced from local farmers and sustainable suppliers, embracing the farm-to-fork movement to reduce our carbon footprint and support our community. Whether you join us for brunch, lunch, or dinner, you can enjoy delicious meals while contributing to a greener future.

Our talented chef and bar team lead the way with eco-friendly practices such as nose-to-tail and root-to-fruit cooking. This approach ensures that every part of the ingredient is used, resulting in high-quality dishes that are not only flavorful but also environmentally conscious. From fresh produce to responsibly sourced proteins, our menu offers a variety of sustainable dining options for our guests to enjoy.

Our bar staff follows suit, incorporating shared ingredients from the kitchen into our creative cocktail recipes. By minimizing waste and using eco-friendly ingredients, we ensure that our craft cocktails are as sustainable as they are refreshing. Whether you're sipping on a signature drink during happy hour or enjoying a late-night cocktail, every effort is made to reduce waste and minimize harmful byproducts.

By choosing to dine at Darling Aviary, you actively participate in our sustainability and conservation efforts. We are proud to collaborate with local suppliers, farmers, and our community to create a positive environmental impact. Join us for a memorable dining experience that supports both your palate and the planet.

OLD SACRAMENTO / OLD SAC / OLD TOWN
www.oldsacramento.com

Old Sacramento is the riverfront historic district, with Gold Rush-era buildings, cobblestone streets, and horse-drawn carriages. It's home to numerous museums, including the Sacramento History Museum and the state Railroad Museum, which offers excursion train rides. Souvenir shops sell T-shirts, movie memorabilia, and antiques, and there are several upscale restaurants and a few bars popular with the college crowd.

FRANKIE'S PIZZA
www.frankiespizzaoldsac.com

Frankie's pizza is a family-owned dream. What started out as Frank's love for pizza quickly became a 30+ year passion of his throughout the years of working in the pizza industry. When Franks first daughter Marissa was born, he quickly became the family man with a dream of owning his own pizza restaurant one day. He even taught Marissa how to make pizza dough at age 4! Although, she was only interested in playing with it.

Every soccer party, birthday party, get together was at a pizza restaurant.

As the years went by, Frank's family grew. Marissa now has 6 younger siblings, but this dream of theirs was still something they always talked about. As the dream got closer to obtain, this father/daughter duo decided to take the leap. The location was perfect, the timing seemed right, and we are extremely excited to bring a new restaurant to town. From our family to yours, we hope Frankie's pizza becomes your favorite place to make new memories.

FRANK FAT'S

www.frankfats.com

Frank Fat's is more than a restaurant; it's a culinary institution, a pillar of the community, a quintessential American success story. Located in the heart of downtown Sacramento—just a few blocks from the State Capitol building—James Beard America's Classic award winner Frank Fat's has been bringing Sacramento's movers and shakers together since 1939.

Started by an immigrant dishwasher, Frank Fat's single-handedly created a downtown political scene, along with a tradition of legendary modern Chinese cuisine and unparalleled service. Come discover why the oldest family-owned restaurant in Sacramento has been thriving for over seventy-five years.

JOHN C. FREMONT PARK

www.exploremidtown.org/yourway/activation-area-fremont-park/

Welcome to Fremont Park, a lively urban oasis in Midtown. This family-friendly park offers a playground, free Wi-Fi, and captivating public art. Throughout the year, enjoy events like Midtown's Second Saturday, fitness programs, concerts, festivals, and movie nights. Discover eight art-covered electrical pedestals and vibrant sculptures by local artist Melissa Uroff. Nearby, find dining and coffee options like Temple Coffee, Magpie Cafe, Karma Brew, Ramen 101, and Orchid Thai for a picnic in the park day.

LAKE NATOMA

www.recreation.gov/gateways/2280

Recreation at Lake Natoma is managed by the California Department of Parks and Recreation under agreement with the Bureau of Reclamation. The Lake was created by Nimbus Dam across the American River. Lake Natoma is a regulating reservoir for releases from Folsom Lake. The Dam and Lake are features of the Central Valley project. Usually open 7 days per week, summer hours (April 1-October 15) are 6:00 a.m. to 9:00 p.m. Winter hours (October 16 - March 30) are 7:00 a.m. to 7:00 p.m. Facilities include one group campground, 11 miles of paved bicycle trails, 6 miles of multi-use trails and excellent year-round bank or boat fishing. Two launch ramps provide continuous boat launching access year-round, in addition to one car-top boat launch area. Lake Natoma is an excellent facility for non-motorized boat recreation. Motorized boating is also allowed and there is a 5 mph speed limit on the entire lake. Good fishing for both cold and warm water species including rainbow trout, brown trout, black bass, crappie and bluegill.

GOLFLAND SUNSPLASH

www.golfland.com/roseville/

Welcome to Northern California's #1 destination for family fun! Golfland-Sunsplash features over 30 exciting rides and attractions in one location! From thrilling waterslides, to award winning miniature golf, Golfland Sunsplash has something for the whole family! We can't wait to see you here! We are easy to find just north of Sacramento in Roseville!

FOLSOM, CA

visitfolsom.com/

Welcome to Folsom, the perfect destination for those seeking urban adventure and a taste of California's great outdoors. You'll find miles of trails, two lakes and a river, exciting history, world-class shopping, arts, theater, dining, and more here. Whether you're seeking a relaxing morning kayaking, the challenge of a bike race or marathon run, an afternoon of retail therapy, or a day of checking out historical attractions, it's easy to choose your own adventure in Folsom.

BJ CINNAMON

https://visitfolsom.com/places/bj-cinnamon/

BJ Cinnamon is a family-owned bakery popularly known for its "fresh out of the fryer and oven" unique signatures cinnamon buns, noted the best in town by locals with a high rating on Yelp. Coffee, tea, pastries, muffins and lines of donuts sold by the dozen in a classic pink box. Huge fresh strawberry eclairs, maple bacon bars, seasonal Fritters, French Cruller pastries, cream puffs, breakfast sandwiches are just a few of the other delicious freshly baked goodness they may have stocked the morning you come in. Line at the door when they open are common!

9 798999 768056